"Life's not been the same since I last saw you."

He stilled. "It hasn't?"

"No," she said somberly. "Thanks to you I'm scarred for life." With a theatrical flourish, she pointed to her nose. "I got three new freckles."

"Freckles," he said blankly. "You got freckles."

"Three," she nodded. "From the sun."

He snorted and leaned back on the bench, his smile crocodile wide.

She grinned back. "You obviously aren't aware of how serious this is."

He laughed—too long, too infectiously. Then he suddenly sobered, half groaning and rubbing his chest with the heel of his hand. "Hell, for a moment there I thought you were going to tell me something way worse."

"What could be worse?" she asked mock-incredulously.

"I thought you were going to tell me you were pregnant."

Pregnant

Kelsi laug
schoolgir

But as th‌‌‌‌‌‌‌‌‌‌‌‌‌‌‌‌‌‌‌‌‌‌‌‌‌‌‌‌‌‌‌‌‌‌ her brain
ticked over slowly. Her g‌‌‌‌‌‌‌‌ o cardiac arrest.

Possibly the only librarian who got told off herself for talking too much, **NATALIE ANDERSON** decided writing books might be more fun than shelving them—and, boy, is it that! Especially writing romance—it's the realization of a lifetime dream, kick-started by many an afternoon spent devouring Grandma's Harlequin® romance novels.

She lives in New Zealand, with her husband and four gorgeous but exhausting children. Swing by her website anytime—she'd love to hear from you at www.natalie-anderson.com.

WALK ON THE WILD SIDE

NATALIE ANDERSON

~ ONE HOT FLING ~

TORONTO NEW YORK LONDON
AMSTERDAM PARIS SYDNEY HAMBURG
STOCKHOLM ATHENS TOKYO MILAN MADRID
PRAGUE WARSAW BUDAPEST AUCKLAND

Recycling programs
for this product may
not exist in your area.

ISBN-13: 978-0-373-52812-7

WALK ON THE WILD SIDE

First North American Publication 2011

WALK ON
THE WILD SIDE

For Dave, for Kathleen, Henry,
Sylvie and Evelyn, and for Mum.

It just wouldn't ever happen without your
patience, support and love.

CHAPTER ONE

ANOTHER red light. Kelsi Reid braked for the fortieth time, muttering beneath her breath as she reached for the comb she'd slung on the passenger seat.

Probably the rest of the clientele came to the salon looking as if they'd just walked out of another—like magazine models, all coiffed, perfumed and perfect. Kelsi hadn't done her hair or make-up. She'd only had time to put in some contacts and wriggle her still-damp-from-the-shower body into her dress.

If only she hadn't fallen asleep at her desk last night as she'd struggled to get all her work done to be able to take today off. If only she hadn't woken up to find her hair trailing in the glass of super sticky, high-energy soda beside her. If only she hadn't frothed the shampoo into such a mass of white bubbles that they'd taken an age to rinse out…

If only she didn't have to go at all.

With the beginnings of a caffeine withdrawal headache, she'd hit every single red light on the way to Merivale—the poshest suburb in Christchurch—the home of L'Essence Spa, and the appointment she'd felt too guilty to be able to cancel.

If only she didn't feel like such a fraud.

Her coworkers and boss had booked it for her. Paid

for it. A combi birthday present/reward for working so hard. Lovely thought but the last thing she wanted. She hated mixing it with the beautiful women—because she was so not one of them. With her horrendous colouring combined with her short stature and the minimal curves that only just stopped her from looking completely boyish, she'd suffered years of taunts as a teen—the freak with the father who hadn't wanted to bother with her either. Fabulous combination made all the more annoying given it had been he who'd donated the gross colour gene in the first place.

She'd got such an inadequacy thing going she'd actually let her old boyfriend take her to a hairdresser and then shopping afterwards so he could purchase her a whole new look—but she'd still not been pretty enough for him. Years later she still couldn't believe she'd let a guy take control of her appearance like that.

In the end she'd rebelled—people thought she looked weird? She'd give them weird. She dressed differently— covering up her almost unnaturally pale skin, covering up her undersized assets, hiding her hair, her eyes, herself. If a man was going to want her, it would be for her mind, or her sense of humour, or fascinating personality or something.

Not that she'd had a date in ages. But she was too busy with work anyway. And it didn't help that her coworkers— the only people she actually knew in this town—were in love with the girls with big guns and even bigger boobs who were the heroines of all the computer games they were so addicted to. In other words, not real.

Kelsi couldn't compete with the living, breathing beauties of this world, let alone the male fantasy ones, so she didn't even try.

But all her workmates—and all of them were male—had

thought this was the sort of thing any woman would want—a day of beauty pampering. She knew they'd meant it kindly. They didn't know about the guy who'd stood and watched every snip of the hairdresser's scissors trying to shape her into something he thought was more attractive. Now she cut her hair herself.

Yet she hadn't the heart to tell them she didn't want it. She knew how exclusive and expensive that salon was, how well intentioned they'd been. And, hey, there were options other than haircuts and spray-tans—full body massage being the one that had really appealed. And a professional wax was always welcome.

So here she was. Going there. But even though she'd toned down her clothing for the day, she was still a misfit— with really knotty, home-dyed hair. And she was running late.

She drove the one hundred metres or so to the next set of traffic lights. They were annoyingly close together here in the middle of the city. And they were red again. Of course.

She lifted her arm and targeted the biggest mess of knots at the back of her head. The bird's nest of unruly curls sprang into being any moment it was freed from the product she religiously used. She had a tube of it in her bag and she'd swipe some in as soon as she could get the comb clear through. But that was apparently impossible today. She bent her head forward and ruthlessly pulled on the comb, screwing her eyes shut as it hurt. Yeah, not good for the hair that was so temperamental anyway, but she had no choice. But as she gave an extra vicious tug her whole body jerked—including her foot, which had been pushing hard on the brake. It slipped right off the pedal. The car slid forward half a metre.

Right into the pedestrian crossing the road.

Kelsi heard the thump. She heard the cut off curse. She heard her own shriek.

She slammed her foot back on the brake and the car jerked. She gripped the steering wheel with both hands, for a split second frozen, shock riveting her to the seat.

The only thing moving was her stomach—rocking violently, its contents swirling round and round and about to be fired up. She flung open the door and tried to race out. The seat belt yanked her back and she banged her hand on the clasp as she fumbled to release it. Finally she got free, slamming the door and running to the front of her car, terrified about what she was going to see. She couldn't feel her legs, couldn't think, couldn't bear it. Had she just killed someone?

'Are you OK? Are you OK? Oh, God.' She struggled to breathe. 'Are you OK?'

'I'm OK.'

It was a man and he was back to standing. Very tall in fact and definitely still alive because his eyes were open—and an incredibly vibrant blue—and he was breathing. Which was more than she was managing at the moment.

Horrified, she shook her head, unable to believe what had just happened. 'I didn't see you.'

'The pedestrian light was green,' he said dryly.

'You just appeared out of nowhere.' Surely she should have seen him earlier? He was over six feet. Hell, if she'd missed him, had there been anyone else? Was there someone stuck under her car right now? She bent and looked under the wheels.

'Your car is fine.'

'I don't care about that,' she said as she frantically searched. 'Was there just you? I didn't hit anyone else?'

She craned her neck to look up at him again.

'Just me.'

'Oh, thank God. I mean…' She gulped, her heart galloping faster. '…you're really OK?'

'Really OK.' He actually laughed. 'Look, you want to move your car? You're holding up the traffic.'

Dazed, she turned and looked at the line of cars behind hers. But most were now moving into the next lane to get around her. So that was OK. Besides, what did a little delayed traffic matter? This was an *accident* scene. She turned back to him. 'Are you sure you're OK?' Her voice rose to a pitch usually only dogs could hear.

He pointed to the footpath. 'Let's talk there.'

Numbly she took a few steps, but stopped sharply, appalled when she saw him walk. 'Oh, no, you're limping. Why are you limping? Where did I get you? Where does it hurt?'

'No, it's just my knee, it's—'

'Your knee?' Her voice rose another three octaves. 'That's where I got you? Oh, let me check.' She dropped to her haunches, reaching out to lift the hem of the long grey shorts he was wearing so she could inspect the damage. She half expected to see screeds of blood coursing down his shin. But there weren't. Instead she was confronted with tanned, muscular calves. Her hand hovered, but the next second he'd stepped out of reach.

'It's fine.' His large hand encircled her upper arm and gently tugged her upwards.

Reluctantly she stood. 'Are you sure?' Had she knocked him right over? She didn't even know. She shuddered as she relived that thudding sound. She'd never had a car accident. Never ever. And now she'd run someone over. 'You don't need a doctor? Please let me take you to the doctor. I think I should take you to a doctor.'

'I don't need a doctor,' he said firmly. 'But you've gone even paler.'

Her stomach heaved more violently as the reality sank in. She slapped her hand to her mouth. 'I could have killed you.'

'You could have. But you didn't.'

She could have killed a child, though. Worst-case scenarios flooded her mind—if it had been a toddler walking next to its mother, or a woman with a pram... It was only luck that had made it a six-foot-however-many-inches giant of a man. And even then she'd hurt him. She stared up at him, her eyes blurring, puffing more than when she ran up the thousand stairs to get to her office on the top floor of the building. She'd hurt him...

Both his hands settled on her shoulders. Firmly. 'It's OK. It was nothing.' He smiled and nodded his head as he emphasised each word.

She swallowed. He really was OK? His grip on her was certainly strong and vital and brought her thoughts to a complete halt.

'You were in a hurry to get somewhere?' he asked.

'What? Yes.' She glanced at her watch and his hands dropped. 'Oh. No.' Way too late now.

'Where?'

'It doesn't matter. It absolutely doesn't matter.' And it didn't. 'Let me take you wherever you were going.' She turned and opened the passenger door and pushed him to get in. 'I'm so sorry I hit you. And you're limping—can I take you to a doctor?'

'No.'

But she wasn't listening. Instead she pushed him harder, wanting him to get into her car, determined to take him, just to make sure. But it was like trying to move a mountain—impossible. And this mountain wasn't cold, it was warm and broad and very, very solid. Not to mention broad—had she registered that already? She slid her palms wider across the inviting breadth, felt the solidness go even more taut—the powerful muscles suddenly snapped with energy.

His flinch brought her back to reality. OMG she had her hands all over his chest.

'Sorry.' Totally flustered she looked up, her gaze instantly caught and locked by his. His eyes were brilliant sky-blue and his smile shone like the brightest sun. Reality vanished again as in a heartbeat she was lost in the gleaming warm intensity. Heavenly blue, most definitely heavenly. She couldn't blink, couldn't breathe, couldn't think of anything but summer warmth and fun and absolute dreaminess...

She blinked. This was *insane*. She'd almost run him over—what was she doing staring at him as if she'd never seen a man before?

Well, she hadn't, at least not one as built as this. Not ever. The only men she saw were those at work and they were all either weedy or obese. Sure, it was a stereotype, but in Kelsi's world it was actually true—computer geek guys were not gorgeous.

This man before her was most definitely not a computer geek. He had to spend serious hours outside to get both a tan like that and muscles like those, not to mention the sun-lightened streaks at the front of his dark brown hair. Hair that hung over his forehead in a casual style begging to be brushed back by her itchy fingers.

He was all utterly natural gorgeousness. But perhaps not, perhaps it was her contacts making him seem so vibrant. What colour tint had she put in today? She couldn't remember. Had one of them slipped? She blinked again. Tried to marshal her far-flung-on-the-breeze thoughts.

'Tell you what, why don't I drive you?' The question

was asked so gently she wasn't sure if he'd actually said it or if she was dreaming.

'Pardon?' She shivered.

His hand lifted to her shoulder again, his thumb stroked her skin, a slow sweep and what she thought he'd just said fled from her head. She shivered again—but she certainly wasn't cold.

'I'm going to drive,' he said very slowly.

He was what? All she knew was that he was smiling and the world was technicolor.

'Come on.'

He seemed to be trying to calm *her* down. She didn't need calming down—she was fine, right? But she was moving, being guided into her own passenger seat by the warm, firm hand on her lower back.

She sat.

'Um.' No point arguing now. He'd shut the door and was walking to the driver's side. She winced as she saw his limp again. This was crazy—she needed to get a grip on herself and apologise once more. She needed to be helping him, not the other way round.

As soon as he got in she asked him, 'Are you sure you're OK to drive?'

There was a half-laugh in reply. It was a nice laugh—low and very, very amused. 'What's your name?'

Kelsi stared at him, the echo of the laugh reverberating through the small space. He looked ridiculous in her car, his knees almost up to his ears. That was because the driver's seat was pushed as far forward as it could go so her feet could reach the pedals. He pushed the seat back to the limit, but even so. The size of him was overwhelming. And he'd said something, hadn't he? Because he was staring back at her expectant-like.

'Sorry?' Her brain had gone far, far offshore into the wide blue yonder.

'Your name?' He leaned across her seat, his torso coming in ultraclose. In a second that strong, broad chest almost touched hers. The action totally struck her dumb—not to mention rendered her immobile. Her body tightened, but not from fear. Oh, no, not fear. This close she could see his symmetrical face, with the hint of shadow on the angular jaw, the gleaming white teeth. She could even feel his heat and he smelt crisp and fresh. She held her breath as he came even closer—was he about to kiss her? Was she going to let this complete stranger kiss her? Mesmerised, she stared into his eyes, his smiling, promise-of-paradise eyes...

Why, yes. Of course she was. There was absolutely no other option she could think of. She couldn't think at all...

But there was a noise right by her ear. Oh. Disappointment crushed as he pulled the seat belt across her body, carefully clicking it into place. Of course he wasn't going to kiss her. Guys like him could kiss a bevy of beauties. He'd never think to kiss her. Oh, but how she'd wanted him to.

Limply she sagged back against the seat. Man, she needed to get a grip. But in the thin summer dress she was wearing, her body had gone all goose-bumpy.

He started the engine and after a moment she peeled her gaze from his big hands on the wheel to watch where they were going. He turned right when she would have gone straight ahead. But it didn't matter.

'Miss?'

Miss? She'd never been called 'miss' by anyone. 'Kelsi.' She finally clued in to what he'd been asking.

'Kelsi, I'm Jack.'

'Hi,' she said vaguely, her brain going AWOL again as she looked at him. Ruthlessly she tried to drag it back to full-attention mode. Kelsi loved surrealist art, but she wasn't sure she was ready for her life to go totally surreal. And having a guy like this driving her who knew where, was definitely surreal.

He laughed again and a dimple creased his jaw giving him a very cheeky look. 'I think you need some recovery time.'

'I'm so sorry.' She sighed and made herself look just slightly to the left of him—so she could try to keep her thoughts on track. He was right. She did need to recover, but not over the accident. It was his gorgeousness and his proximity that were screwing up her thought processes now. 'Are you sure you're OK?'

He lifted one hand from the wheel, holding it up in the 'stop' sign. 'Don't start that again. Please.'

'Right.' She nodded. Yeah. She'd hardly been cool, calm and collected. Not at all the kind of person you'd want to be in an emergency. She'd been a jibbering mess.

'I know a café that does fantastic coffee,' he said. 'Let's get some, OK?'

Coffee. That was her problem. She hadn't had her hit this morning. That was why she was feeling both so wired and wobbly now—not the accident, not him.

He pulled into a car park and killed the engine.

'You can't park here, it's reserved.' Customer only spaces for the snow'n'skate-wear store—the signs were everywhere.

He didn't even glance at them. 'They won't mind.'

He was Mr Laid-back wasn't he? Did he take everything in his stride—literally in his stride—like being hit by however many tonnes of metal car? He grinned and pocketed her keys as he limped onto the footpath beside her. She tried not to stare but the guilt seized her. Then his hand seized her upper arm even more firmly and he swung her round, walking her into the doorway of the cool café.

'Sit.' He stopped at the closest table. 'I'm getting you a coffee.'

Kelsi plopped into the chair and put her elbow on the table, closing her eyes as she rested her head in her hand. 'A black coffee would be fantastic.' Coffee would kick her back together—because this brainless behaviour could no longer be her.

Jack paused and looked at the paler-than-pale petite woman in front of him. You'd think she'd been the one hit by the car, not him. Truth be told he'd hardly been touched, had thumped his fist on the bonnet and dodged to avoid it. But doing that had wrenched his weak knee—hence the worsening of the limp. The surgery had been a couple of weeks ago, but right now it felt as if it had been yesterday.

He walked to the counter, trying to stretch out the soreness the sudden movement had caused, hoping it wasn't going to set his progress back. He was desperate to get training again.

He ordered from Viv, the barista, but she had his half made already and it took nothing for her to make another. So in seconds he was heading back to the dangerous driver, two steaming cups in hand. Beneath his breath he chuckled as he looked at her slim back and the wild mess that was her hair—she had no idea, did she?

He put the drinks on the table, ripped open three sachets of sugar and tipped them into the first cup. He stirred the liquid round a bit with a spoon and then pushed the cup towards her.

'I don't take sugar.' A weak smile as she slumped against the back of the seat.

'You do today.' Strong, hot and sweet. It was exactly what she needed.

He watched while she took a sip—one, then a much bigger gulp. Then she exhaled.

'Better?' He couldn't help laughing.

'Much.'

Yeah, her crazy-coloured eyes were focused now, and she sat up straight. That was also good because when she'd been flopped back like that, the thin strap of her dress had slipped. He'd seen the lacy edging of a pretty black bra and he shouldn't be thinking about sex this second. But he was—and had been the last six hundred seconds, or so. Ever since he'd first laid eyes on her.

Not appropriate. That wasn't why he'd insisted on getting her a coffee. No, he'd done that because he wanted to let her know she hadn't done any damage. He'd seen the guilt on her face as he'd walked towards her—she thought she'd done that to his knee. He needed to relieve her of that burden because, despite her alternative, all-black, all-attitude couture, she was the type to have nightmares about it for weeks. A little bit of sweetness wrapped up in 'wannabe different' city slicker sophistication.

But first, there was something else he had to tend to. He stood, barely resisting the urge to laugh again, and walked round the table. She stiffened as he touched her.

'Easy,' he murmured. 'You'll make it worse.'

The comb was well and truly caught—knotted in the mass of curls at the back of her head. She hadn't realised, of course, and he heard her gasp as she did now. Amusement washed over him and he wanted to make her laugh about it, too. Except she was too busy blushing. Seeing the colour in her cheeks was good, hearing her breathing quicken was even better. So he affected her?

Excellent. Because he was still suffering from a severe

lust attack. He tried to concentrate on the tangled bit of plastic but up this close he found out her hair was extremely curly and shockingly blonde and also soft and smelt flower sweet. Like her eyes, the colour was fake, but her natural shade must be reasonably light because there wasn't any darkness showing at the roots. Or maybe she'd just had it done. Jack was used to blondes and their high-maintenance hair, but he'd never seen blonde as snow white as this. Or as messy.

He swallowed, his mouth dry, as he bent closer to free her hair from the comb without hurting her. Her scent was all he could taste. She turned him on as if he hadn't been turned on in a long while—and Jack was no stranger to sex.

Well, not usually. The knee op had put paid to any and all kinds of fun for a while—both on the snow and in the bedroom. That must be the reason for this intense reaction to this woman, right? Because petite pieces of fragility like her didn't usually do it for him. He was into strong, athletic women who could match his needs, not slim things who looked as if they'd blow over in a light wind.

And he definitely wasn't into overly emotional women. No to neediness, thanks very much—his lifestyle didn't let him offer much to anyone, certainly not much in the way of emotional support. But when he'd seen the softness of her soul in those moments when she'd thought she'd hurt him, that womanly sweetness had been achingly tempting—the blinking back of the tears and the trembling lips. Yeah, her lips. Their crushed-rose colour—unlike so much else of her—was natural. Neither a glossy nor matte finish adorned them. They were full and deep and inviting all on their own.

He'd badly wanted to kiss her feelings better.

He wanted to do more than kiss her now. He was

imagining scooping her up in his arms—it'd be so easy, and so delightful to nibble on the delicacies hidden under that to-the-floor, funeral-march-style dress.

He was in for an even longer spell of abstinence. That was the problem. Knowing he had another four weeks ahead of him with no chance of getting any had put sex at the forefront of his brain. That was why he was struggling to control his body in the middle of a busy café. That was why he was attracted to a woman as wrong a playmate for him as a piranha was as wrong a tank buddy for an angelfish.

Carefully he worked the comb free. It took longer than he'd thought it would but he didn't mind. He hadn't known he had a touch of the masochist in him. That he'd *like* the torture of his fingers brushing accidentally against her and not touching how he really wanted to. He throbbed with the temptation to run his fingers right through and muss up her hair even more. Yeah, the upcoming physical rehab session was making him wild-dog horny. He gritted his teeth and tried to concentrate on the job, not on the urges thudding through his blood.

Impossible. Pale, soft, striking, she sat like a statue before him, her embarrassment radiating out. But there was more to the heat, wasn't there?

Jack was used to being wanted. He enjoyed being wanted—to be pleased and to please. So he knew the signs. Sometimes he ignored them, sometimes he didn't.

But now his knee had stopped its death-pain throbbing, he knew he was going to succumb to the most debilitating bout of temptation he'd ever experienced. Even though it was probably inappropriate, he couldn't resist. He liked the unexpected. He liked a challenge. He liked to live on the edge.

So what if he had less than twenty-four hours? So what

if he should be in some boring meeting? That made it all the more delicious. Jack Greene knew how to make the most of every minute.

CHAPTER TWO

KELSI just couldn't look Jack in the eye as he waved the comb in front of her before placing it on the table. She barely mumbled her thanks as he sat back down in the chair opposite her.

So she was too late for her appointment at the super spa. So she'd had a lime-green comb caught in the back of her hair. So she'd run over a prime piece of male. So she'd nearly hyperventilated when that prime piece had stood so close and so carefully got that comb out and all she'd been able to think about was how tall he was and how gentle, despite the way he was *built*...

So now she really wanted to leave. Except she had almost run him over, and, instead of her making it up to him, *he'd* driven her to a nice café, bought her coffee and encouraged her to relax. So she couldn't skip out on him. She had to stay—just to be polite, right? Her internal debate was pointless anyway—he still had her car keys.

She looked at him and fell apart inside again. The gleam in his eyes was even brighter now and he definitely gave her the complete once-over, and did he linger on her lips? Kelsi fought against her immediate instinct to run her tongue over them—she was *not* going to be so obvious. Not, not, not. *Especially* because he was so gorgeous. Without doubt he was used to having some kind of mesmerising effect on females because that confident, cheeky smile was spreading over his face.

Instead of licking her lips she took another sip of coffee. The warmth braced her and sent the last of the cold, sick feeling from the accident packing. As she swallowed, her brain clicked back to fully functioning—*finally*.

She figured if she didn't look him in the eye she could maybe keep her brain working. But looking at his body wasn't that much better. Mentally she tried to box him up so she could put him away—but he needed one that she didn't have in the 'overwhelming male' compartment of her brain. He was a bit too big and fit and breathtaking…

She inhaled deeply, determined to make a polite, hopefully sane, effort. She totally owed him that. He flashed the ultracharm smile again but she was smart and looked at her coffee cup instead. Only another mouthful and it'd be finished. Then she could go.

'So, what were you late for?' he asked as she lifted the cup.

She lowered it, feeling the heat rising in her cheeks. 'Nothing.'

His brows lifted. 'Not nothing. Tell me.'

OK, so now he was going to think she was a total sad ditz. 'A spa treatment.'

'A what?' he asked, sounding a little too confused.

Kelsi was sure he'd heard but he was just making her say it again because she was so flushed. Pointlessly, she tried to smooth her hair behind her ear.

'A spa,' she said, determined to speak clearly. 'You know, a day treatment at a beauty parlour.' Not just any parlour, the most exclusive salon in town. They obviously thought she really needed it—this guy probably did, too.

'And what were you having done?'

'Facial, massage, hair.' She shrugged and lifted the cup to her mouth.

'Cut or wax?'

She nearly choked on the coffee. 'Cut.' She tried to lie like a pro but she knew her colour had risen higher. The nerve of him.

He was grinning wildly now. Openly laughing at her plans for the day and stupidly she felt the need to justify it—even when it hadn't been her idea. 'I haven't had a day off in four months. My boss said I needed to recharge my batteries.'

'A beauty salon wouldn't be the place to do that.'

No. She'd have picked an art gallery. Preferably one in Paris. One day she'd get to do the travel thing—once she had her career established.

'What about some fresh air? A walk somewhere nice? Wouldn't that be more of a boost?'

Of course he would be the outdoor sports guy—the sport billy, with a practically-kill-yourself-climbing-a-mountain-to-feel-good approach to life. She couldn't think of anything worse. She just wanted to relax—and rest. 'Fresh air isn't good for my skin,' she said with a helpless gesture.

'No?'

Was the man blind? She was practically albino. Well, not really—the hundreds of freckles proved her pigment worked all right. She felt her flush deepen. 'I burn really easily.'

'You could wear a hat,' he drawled.

She opened her eyes ingénue wide and batted her lashes as she drawled right back at him, 'And ruin my hair?'

His gaze rested on the tangle and then sliced into hers again. A split second of solemnity froze them both.

And then they laughed—simultaneously, genuinely. She

shook her head at her lame little joke. But the amusement warmed her veins better than the energising coffee she'd just swallowed.

'Tell you what, Ms Spa Treatment, seeing you've lost your day at the salon, let me take you out instead. We'll see how much better you feel after some fresh air.'

She met the inviting blue pools that were his eyes and couldn't ignore the tingling sensation spreading over her skin. Had she bumped her head in that accident and not realised? Because she was thinking all kinds of weird thoughts now—such as that this guy might actually be hitting on her. And that just couldn't be possible. 'Um...'

'Come on, come and have some fun.'

'It isn't fun outdoors.'

'You're afraid.' The smallest hint of provocation sharpened his gaze.

'No,' she denied, 'I'm just not...' Believing this guy had just asked her out. 'Interested.'

'Really?' His voice dropped to a whisper. 'Not even a little bit?'

She swallowed. He knew he was gorgeous, didn't he? But before she could think up even a vaguely suitable reply, he tweaked her nerves that bit harder.

'You don't like a challenge?'

'You're seriously suggesting that a day outdoors would be better than a day at a spa.' She finally managed to answer, amazed her voice didn't break like a teen boy's.

'A million times better.'

'That's quite some promise.' She sipped the last drop of her coffee and wrinkled her nose as she got the bitter bits.

'You're going to take me up on it?'

She avoided his eyes as she thought about it. Really, it was a no-brainer. She couldn't bear the thought of going to the spa and apologising for her tardiness now. And she couldn't go to work. As the only female designer, Kelsi felt a certain pressure to do better than the boys, but working extreme hours on a deadline had left her jaded and in need of a break—something her boss had noticed, hence the spa thing. She couldn't let them know she hadn't showed up.

And what else would she do? She'd been working so hard since moving here she hadn't had time to build a huge social life out of work. Honestly, she hadn't built much of a social life at work either—her new computer-boy colleagues were all into gaming and she wasn't. That pretty much ended it. But she was quite sure Jack didn't have social life issues. He was in a whole other league altogether—handsome, charming, bound to be a player. 'You don't have anything better to do?'

'Not right now. No.'

Her body was the ice cream, temptation the raspberry ripple—churning right through and flavouring every bit of herself. 'What's in it for you?'

'The pleasure of seeing you cross over to the light side.'

'The outdoor appreciation society, you mean?'

'We might need to get something better for you to wear, though.' His gaze narrowed.

She stiffened—was he about to tell her what she should wear?

'I thought girls were over the Goth phase by the time they hit their twenties.' He smiled, skewering her on two fronts—with his gleaming expression and teasing words.

But Kelsi's swift flash of anger got doused by that expression. If her instincts were on track, he didn't think her outfit was all that ugly.

'I'm not Goth,' she said, feeling his eyes burning

through her—making her body respond in a far too physical way.

'Emo then. The whole vampire thing, isn't it?' he asked softly. 'Pale skin and weird-coloured eyes and loose dark clothes.'

Kelsi clasped her hands together in front of her body, hiding the tightness of her nerves—and nipples. 'I am not on the vampire bandwagon. I change my hair and eye colour all the time. And the pale skin I can't help.' The loose dark clothing accusation she had to admit to—but she had reason. 'Covering up protects it from the sun.'

She watched him look her over once more and half wished she were wearing her usual ten layers or so instead of just the one long dress. In fact, its spaghetti straps and thin, clinging fabric meant she was far more exposed than usual.

'See, you are a vampire.' He grinned suddenly, wickedly. 'Concealing yourself.'

'I'm *re*vealing myself.' She laughed at his ridiculousness. 'It's self-expression. I work in a creative industry.'

'What, so you have to look as way out as possible? With dyed hair and unnatural eyes?' He leant forward, penetrating. 'What's their real colour anyway?'

She flexed her fingers, moving to disperse some energy. 'Nothing exciting.'

'No?'

'Some people accessorise with handbags or shoes or both. I accessorise with eye colour or pattern.'

'Pattern?' His brows shot up. 'Patterns on your eyes?'

'Sure.' She had the most fabulous collection of freaky contacts. Shopping on the internet was a temptation to which she frequently succumbed.

'Why?'

'Why not?' It was different. It wasn't the typical beautiful babe thing—she wasn't ever going to be pretty or beautiful. She couldn't compete with that—but she could do quirky. She could do defence.

'You're like an inverse chameleon. You hope people won't see past the surface?' He nailed her just like that. He finished his coffee and stood. 'Come on, then, so long as you're sure you're not going to eviscerate if you go into the sunshine, let's get out of here.'

It wasn't the sun that threatened to eviscerate her. It was his burning focus.

On the footpath outside he tossed the car keys at her. 'I just need to get something. Be a minute.'

She caught the keys and watched him walk unevenly across the road into the snow'n'skate store.

This was her opportunity to escape him—to get in the car and put her foot on the accelerator to the spa and apologise for lateness. But as if she was going to do that—she hadn't wanted to go there anyway. And as if she was going to pass up an opportunity to spend some time with a good-humoured guy who looked as if he'd just stepped out of a sportswear catalogue?

She might be different, but she wasn't crazy.

She got into the car and scooted the driver's seat forward again so her feet could reach the pedals. He was back in a minute as he'd said, clutching an uber-hip recyclable shopping bag with the store's logo.

'You have friends in there?'

He just winked, chucking the bag on the back seat and fixing the legroom in the passenger seat. 'You sure you're OK to drive?'

With a flourish she curled her fingers round the steering wheel. 'I'm fine.'

He leaned close. 'No more urgent grooming matters to attend to?' His voice was the auditory equivalent of chocolate sauce—warm and smooth and ready for a berry to be dipped in it.

'I think the pedestrian population is safe now,' she muttered, trying to get her pulse to stop its rapid acceleration.

'Great. Then take the first left.'

She did exactly that and in only a hundred metres or so had to stop—a red light. Naturally. But as she paused he leaned across her seat, reaching his long arm down between her legs.

'What are you doing?' she gasped. 'I'm trying to drive.' She lifted both hands from the wheel, undecided if she should throttle him—his head was basically in her lap!

'Stop it.' Actually she didn't mean that. She was thinking all kinds of things she shouldn't be, what with seeing his dark head hovering just above her thigh like that…

Not wriggling was really difficult. So was not crashing the car. 'We're at a red light. I'm trying to concentrate.'

And that was so impossible right now. He moved his hand, his shoulder rubbed against her thigh as he jerked on the handbrake between them. Then he went south again— deep south. His hand encircled her ankle, lifted it for a half second as he slipped her shoe off.

'Jack!' Another totally girly gasp.

He sat back, a smile of success creasing every feature, as her shoe sat in the palm of his hand. 'You can't drive safely wearing these. You can't do anything safely wearing these.'

'I can and do,' she said breathlessly. 'If you were as short as me, and plainly you're not, then you'd understand. As it is, you can't possibly get it.'

'I just want to get there in one piece.'

She blew out a big shot of air and finally realised she had to take the brake off as the car behind tooted impatiently.

Irritatingly, it was easier to drive barefoot—but she wasn't going to admit it to him. 'That was really dangerous.'

'No more dangerous than you combing your hair at a red light. At least this time you had your handbrake on.'

'Where are we going anyway?' She chose to change the subject.

'Straight ahead for now.' He gave her a sideways look that was full of a charming smile. 'Are you OK driving on the hills?'

'Stop trying to get into the driver's seat. I'm fine with hills.' She bit the inside of her cheek. OK, so she wasn't that fine with them, but damned if she was going to let him know that.

'There are a few hairpin corners. I can take over if you want.'

In response she trod harder on the accelerator. In only a few minutes they were heading up the hill out of town towards the peninsula that curved out from the mainland. The hills were barren and brown—no trees or scrub covering them, just tussock that leaned away from the wind. Against the bright blue sky the hills were majestic. She liked their stark smoothness and the contrast against the clear sky and blue water. But then came one of those hairpin turns.

'You want the air conditioning on?'

So he'd noticed she was sweating.

'It doesn't work.' One of the many idiosyncrasies of the car that one day she'd get fixed.

'You should walk in town anyway.'

She sent him a look.

'Carbon footprint,' he said mock piously.

'My heels don't leave much of a footprint anyway.'

He laughed and didn't talk more, didn't need to direct as there was only the one road to follow. And she needed to concentrate and not be further distracted by the giant hunk of man making her car feel like a matchbox toy. But after the worst hill bit she began to relax into it, able to take in the expansive view of bronze earth and blue sky and sparkling water. The silence wasn't uncomfortable. It was nice—as if they were leaving all the clutter and noise of city life behind them.

'So why do your batteries need recharging, Kelsi? What do you do that's made you so worn out?'

'Computers,' she said. 'Website design.'

'You sit in front of a screen all day?'

'And you want to know the shocking thing?' She grinned and touched the accelerator with a heavier tread. 'I like it.'

He shook his head. 'Crazy.'

He told her to take the left when the road forked. The gravel road dipped, leading down to sea level. And then it ended. She pulled in, parking beneath one of the few trees around. She stepped out of the car, uncomfortably hobbling on the one shoe. He got the bag off the back seat and pulled something from it.

'What is that?' She stared at it.

He twirled it on his finger and grinned outrageously. 'It isn't obvious?'

'And you think I'm going to wear it?'

'The store didn't stock sunscreen. And I'm betting you don't have any in that uselessly small bag of yours.'

No, she didn't. Because she always, always, always stayed in the shade. Resigned, she took the wide-brimmed monstrosity of a hat from him and slapped it on her head.

'I have a wrap for your shoulders, too.'

She took the long stretch of cloth and reminded herself to avoid looking in his eyes. They made her want to smile too much. And they were filled with a fire she longed to feel on her flesh. Crazy—she definitely needed a day to recharge.

'I had the feeling you'd like the colour.'

It was jet black. Like every item of clothing she already had on.

'How astute of you.' She wrapped it around her shoulders and walked a few paces. Then she stopped. 'How am I supposed to walk on this?'

'Maybe you should take your other shoe off. Get your feet wet.'

'Get my feet dirty, you mean.' She looked at the sand and barely suppressed a shudder. 'I hate the beach. All the little biting insects come to get me. You can see them circling overhead, ready to dive-bomb and sink their teeth in.'

'You must have sweet blood.'

'Now who's the one sounding like a vampire?' She had to send him an arch look. 'I don't like sand either. It sticks everywhere and my skin gets itchy.'

'Guess we won't be rolling in the waves, then, huh?'

'Pardon?' She stopped walking.

'Surfing,' he explained, the twinkle gleaming brighter in his eyes. 'You don't want to surf? I know where I can get a couple of wetsuits.'

'I don't surf and I definitely don't wear wetsuits.' She shuddered even more obviously.

He laughed. 'Next you'll be telling me you don't even swim in the sea.'

'Never,' she admitted with embarrassment. 'I'd rather be in a private pool.'

'With all those chemicals?'

OK, so she knew she was pathetic. But she couldn't resist sparring with him a little. 'Isn't the sea more polluted?'

'Not this bit of beach.'

She put her hand to her heart in drama academy style. 'But there might be sharks.'

'Or friendly dolphins.'

'Jellyfish.' She fluttered her fingers in his face.

'Starfish and shells to admire.' He caught her hands and held them still in front of him, smiling widely. 'Face it, you can't win on this. Nature might bring its dangers, but its beauty makes them worth the risk.'

Kelsi couldn't think of another argument—too distracted by the marvel of nature right in front of her. What with the sea/sky-blue eyes and the slightly shaggy dark hair and the golden skin, he was quite the gorgeous surfie type. Easygoing and relaxed in nature but with no fat, just pure, lean muscle in his body—she could feel his potential strength even from the light grip he had on her.

Anticipation licked through her. She hadn't been in the company of anyone so attractive in a long, long time. OK, ever.

Pure guy candy.

She suddenly realised she was breathless—almost panting—and they hadn't even begun the slight climb over the sand dune down to the water. She pulled her hands free of his and made herself stop visually feasting on him. It was a wonder she wasn't drooling. She knew she was blushing so she made a show of looking around so he couldn't see the stain rising on her cheeks.

There wasn't another car in the car park, and not another soul on the small curve of beach. No boats in the distance on the horizon. They could have been the only two people on all the earth for all she knew.

It was a surprisingly liberating thought.

When she turned back he kicked off his shoes and pointedly stared at the one left on her foot. She sighed but removed the darn thing, ignoring how nice the soft, warm sand felt as her toes sank into it.

This was crazy. Totally crazy. She was at a remote beach with a complete stranger. She was in the *sun*.

But it was heavenly.

She glanced at him as he strolled easily beside her. His limp was almost imperceptible now—thank goodness. But he was grinning like a wolf who knew everything.

'What?' She pulled herself together and tried to recover her wits.

He laughed then and she knew it was too late—she was already succumbing to the power of the environment. Even though she knew the sand flies were lining up preparing their attack, even though she could already feel the burning power of the sun. What did it matter when her lungs could fill and stretch with fresh, clean air? What did it matter when she was accompanied by a guy who was like a summer sprite—full of fun and sun and sexiness?

The hard ball of stress wedged just above her stomach softened. The office was miles away, computers miles away, *pressure* miles away. Instead there was just the beautiful blue of the sea and the sky stretching as far as she could see. And the warmth under her feet and on her skin thawed the cold inside her, too.

She walked to the edge of the water, aware that a metre or so away he'd taken a few steps into it so the waves lapped over his ankles. She turned away from him, gazing at the bronze hills behind them and back to the deep blue but, all the while, so incredibly aware of the picture of male beauty he made. She walked alongside the edge, listening to the gentle splashes his feet made as he walked two paces to the side and behind her.

'So what's your favourite season, then?' he asked suddenly. 'Winter, right?'

'Yes.' She grinned at her own predictability.

'Mine, too.'

'No way.' Surprised, she turned and walked backwards to look at him.

'Yeah.' He nodded. 'I spend my life chasing winter.'

She frowned. 'But you're so tanned.'

He laughed. 'Because I'm here for the summer recovering.' He bent and rubbed his hand over his knee. 'This is an old injury—you didn't do that with the car before.'

'Really?'

'I had an operation a couple weeks ago. I'm about to go for a rehab stint in Canada. Get back into training.'

'Training for what?'

He grinned a little sheepishly. 'I snowboard.'

She stopped walking altogether. 'For a living?'

'Professional snowboarder. Yes.'

'Seriously?' Wow. No wonder he looked so fit. She had to stifle a giggle. She'd never got this close to a professional athlete before. 'So.' She coughed. 'You're training for the Olympics?'

'The Olympics aren't for a couple more years, there's some other big comps before then but, yes, the Olympics are on the horizon.'

He really was serious? 'Have you been to other Olympics?'

He grinned. OMG he had.

'I went as a demonstration last time but at the next Olympics mine is an official event. The first gold is coming home with me,' he said. The grin had gone—now he was utterly, utterly serious.

And, oh, my, she believed him. 'So you go from season to season—here to Canada?'

'Or France, China.' He nodded. 'Wherever has the best snow.'

'And you work on the ski field or have sponsors or something?'

Surprise flashed in his eyes for a second. She didn't mean to embarrass him, but she didn't think professional snowboarders would get paid all that much. It wasn't exactly football and on the front page all the time.

'Uh, something like that.' He nodded. 'You ever snowboarded?'

She shook her head and turned back to walk along the shoreline.

'Skied?'

'No.'

'But I thought you liked winter.'

'I do.' She wrapped her arms around her waist. 'I like curling up in front of a fire.'

'That's what you do *after* the day on the slopes.'

She mock shuddered again.

'You should try it some time.' His amusement warmed his words. 'You'll see I'm right. Like I'm right about this.'

She heard a big splash and turned in time to see him kick again—sending a spray of water up, splashing the hem of her dress.

'It's not so hard, is it?' he asked.

'What?' She looked at him, the heat deep in her belly bubbling now.

'Admitting defeat.'

She moved towards him, unthinkingly taking a step into the water. It wasn't as cold as she'd expected. So she took another.

Tanned, relaxed, utterly at home, he smiled at her. All confident. All successful. All gorgeous.

And interested. She couldn't believe it but there was no way she was misinterpreting the wickedness in his smile.

No man had ever looked at her with such obvious attraction. Never a man as gorgeous as him.

It was intoxicating—making her feel powerful and beautiful and bolder than she'd ever been in her life. All of a sudden super-vixen urges surged high. Crazy, wanton, wild feelings. And in the madness of the midday sun she let them all out.

'You've made me wet,' she said. Her gaze locked to his, she let him see her willingness. 'But if you're going to do that, you could at least do it properly.'

His brows lifted and the splashes sounded less gentle as he walked closer. His eyes sparkled more blindingly than the reflection of the sun on the water and his smile softened to intimate. His voice was on the same wave—wonderful. 'How wet do you want to get?'

Excitement shot through her, stiffening every muscle. She tilted her head back so she could keep the eye contact as he came right into her space. 'How wet can you make me?'

CHAPTER THREE

JACK's hands moved, the very tips of fingers first caressing her collarbones, then lifting to cup her jaw. 'You want to drown?'

Kelsi already was. In the rampant desire flooding her system. 'Yes,' she whispered.

She closed her eyes against the sun as he bent towards her. His lips merely grazed hers—a light rubbing back and forth—until she parted her mouth more and reached onto tiptoe to demand a heavier pressure.

She got it. His hand shifted to the back of her head, holding her firmly as his tongue delved into her hungry mouth. He stroked her—hot and powerful and with unmistakable purpose. The explicitness only excited her more. The force of her need took her by surprise—roaring through her as he unleashed the sensual strength she'd sensed he had. She'd been attracted to him from the moment she'd recovered enough to actually *see* him after the accident. But even so she hadn't realised the extent of the chemistry she'd feel with him—that any hesitation or caution or modesty would be flung far from her at the first kiss.

'Kelsi,' he muttered, breaking a few millimetres away. 'I fly out to Canada tomorrow.'

'That's nice,' she said, half dazed and desperate to touch her mouth to his again.

He half laughed, half groaned. 'Yeah, but—'

'It's OK, Jack,' she said, stroking his jaw with her fingers. 'Let's just enjoy this afternoon.'

On this beach with its infinite grains of sand and the water that would ebb and flow for ever, she felt as if this afternoon could be as endless as the number of stars in the sky. The fact there'd be no tomorrow was just perfect—there'd be no rejection then either. She'd had too much of that in the past. But she could be free if there was just the here and now.

He looked closely into her eyes, until he was seemingly satisfied with what he saw. As he should be—because it was her total submission to the spark between them. To how wanted he made her feel. And how much she wanted. Her 'on' button had been pushed—but even she hadn't known she was capable of such thermonuclear heat.

He was so tall she had to bend back to kiss him, but that was good because it pushed her body hard against his. She felt the impact of the contact shuddering through every cell. Every nerve pinged with the need to know more of him—all of him—her body hummed for completion.

She rotated her hips, unable to remain still when there was the pleasure of him to be had. He slid his arms right around her, one hand low on her back pushing her even closer, and then he rocked, too, mimicking the movement of sex, making her want their bodies to be sealed—submerged.

In seconds she reached flashpoint. Moaning into his mouth as sexual energy rocketed around her body, desperate for release. He broke apart again and she moaned louder. But he walked around her, pressing kisses on her face and neck as she panted. His fingers traced over her shoulders, playing with the thin straps of her dress. Until he stood behind her, both of them facing out to the horizon.

But she was unable to see it, lost in the sense of intimacy he'd spun around her.

She trembled as he slid his hands up her thighs, taking her dress up with them. She didn't care how outrageous she was being. How fast this was. All she wanted was his touch—everywhere.

Despite the tightness contracting her muscles, her legs wouldn't hold her any more. She leant back against him. Firm hands on her waist pulled her down to her knees, an inch of water washed over her legs—delightfully cool against her burning skin.

'You want to surf something?' He nuzzled the nape of her neck.

She tried to push her knees farther apart to give him better access, but they dug into the wet sand. He'd knelt, too, his front sealed to her back, his thighs framing hers, his erection pressing behind her. She couldn't answer, her breathing shot, so hot, as he kissed over the top of her shoulders. His warm breath skimmed over her chest, teasing her nipples to even tighter nubs.

His big arm curled around her, his forearm pressing against her belly as his hand reached lower, fingers slipping under her dress and then beneath the band of her silk knickers. She shuddered as he went lower still, touching her intimately—gently, slowly finding that swollen spot that was so sensitive. His other hand wrapped around her, too, teasing her breasts—cupping them, gently massaging and then tormenting each taut nipple.

She rocked against him, turning her head back to catch his mouth with hers. She liked the strong kisses, she liked the feeling that she was encircled in his power. He was all around her, and in the prison of his arms she sensed she was about to soar. His caresses were sweet rhythmic torture as he kissed her hard.

She ran her hands over his thighs—spreading her fingers wide over their rock solid strength, rubbing him harder as her excitement grew. His touches quickened in response, and went lower, deeper into her slick heat.

She cried out as he pushed inside. His fingers thrust as she ground down on them in ecstasy. His thumb massaged her clit some more—driving her crazy. She was hot and wet and squirming but it still wasn't enough. Her head fell back, resting on his shoulder. He kissed her neck, sucking, savouring as his fingers plunged and stroked deeper still.

Encompassed by heat and strength and sex, she groaned in pleasure, unable to form the words to beg for what she wanted—for more, all of him, the ultimate intimacy. Her fingers dug into his thighs but it was too late—the pressure built, too much for her to hold, bursting her apart. He held her tight against him as she convulsed, the pleasure coming in violent waves that were too exquisite to endure.

Closing her eyes in the white-hot intensity, she cried out, her raw scream ringing out across the empty beach.

Shuddering, she collapsed back, overwhelmed. Gently he stroked the inside of her thighs, soft swirling touches that sent sparks rippling through her system. It was no longer blood that travelled along her veins, but brilliant light—a kaleidoscope of colour and sensation. And all of it magnificent.

As she floated halfway back to reality she felt the coiled tension in him—iron solidity contrasting with her liquid, languid muscles.

'Feel better now?' he asked softly in her ear.

She had no hope of voicing an answer—no words could express how she felt. No one had ever done that before—no one had held her and focused so purely on her and her needs alone. No one had made her feel so alive. No one had made her feel so fulfilled—and so hungry.

She moved, redrawing her strength, twisting round to look at him. Slowly she shook her head. She said nothing, just crossed her arms over her body, took hold of her dress and pulled it up over her head. She tossed the thin silk up the beach behind him.

Boldly she watched him watch her. She saw his swallow, saw the colour staining his golden skin, saw the sheen of sweat on his forehead, saw the tension in his every muscle. He really did want her.

She was so glad she'd decided to wear her very best matching black bra and knicker set to the beauty salon that morning. Silly how important it seemed to impress another woman—especially one who was about to wax your most private areas. But now she watched with victorious pleasure as his breathing became more ragged as he gazed at the scraps of silk and the detailed lace that made a peek-a-boo show of her nipples. Her breasts pushed tightly against the material and her knickers were drenched—but he knew that already.

She reached forward and lifted the hem of his T-shirt. His breath hissed as he held up his arms so she could get it off him.

'You want it all?' he muttered roughly.

'Yes, please.' She leaned forward and kissed his throat, nuzzling the stubble-roughened skin of his jaw.

'Are you sure?'

She pulled back to look in his eyes. 'Don't you want to?'

'Oh, honey,' he choked on a laugh. 'I want like you wouldn't believe. But don't feel like you have to—'

'Oh, I have to. I absolutely *have* to.' Smiling with relief, she ran her hands over his chest, marvelling at his physique. He was tall and big but not body-builder beefy. Rather he was long and lean. His skin stretched smooth and warm over him—not an ounce of fat beneath, just honed muscles. High Definition in the flesh. And so much better than any onscreen star. He tensed even more as she spread her hands wide over the light sprinkle of hair, the tips of her little fingers teasing ever so lightly over his mouth-watering nipples.

Yes. She wanted like she couldn't believe as well.

She reached up and kissed him, sucking his lip into her mouth, feeling a weird freedom to explore every kind of fantasy with him. Because this was all fantasy now—a fantasy moment on a fantasy beach that she had to make the most of. His hands encircled her waist and she kissed him as if she'd never kissed another—with nothing but passion, hiding none of her need. Not feeling in the least self-conscious or shy or inadequate, just turned on and ready for pure pleasure, pure indulgence.

She knelt closer, pressing on his lap. 'Come on.' She wanted him in her and pounding hard, hard, hard.

'Make me.' His eyes glittered with diamond-bright light.

Anticipation tingled through her at his challenge. How reckless of him—it was more than an invitation to play, she wanted to torture. She wanted to drive him wild. To make him shake and beg for release as he'd made her. And she wanted him to have an orgasm like the one that was still sending aftershocks along her nerves, leaving her with that incredible driving need for more.

He was utterly motionless as she undid the button on his long denim shorts, and unzipped them. His erection sprang free. Commando man, huh? She pushed his chest. He smiled and lay back onto the sand, the water lapping his skin. Astride him in her underwear, she looked down at the embodiment of sensual perfection. He knew what he was doing, he totally knew. An experienced lover. But that was OK, because today she wanted the best. She'd never had the best of experiences in bed, never been brilliant, as her ex had brutally informed her, but now the lingering high from the most awesome orgasm of her life gave her confidence, and from the way Jack's muscles were straining she thought she had a shot at not bad.

So her smile matched his in wickedness. Until she realised she didn't know where to touch, which bit to kiss. She bit her lip, let her finger walk over him to start while she decided. The rippling reaction of his muscles was inspiring—so she let her mouth follow the path. All too soon she knew what she wanted, the crunching urge deep inside her womb fuelled her passionate hunger to take him in her mouth and pleasure him until he'd only be able to see stars—right now. Straight to the joystick.

Her hand clamped round the base of his erection. He groaned as she kissed him. She felt his whole body tense up even more. She licked the head of him, swirling her tongue over the thick ridge. And then she opened up and took him in. He was big, silky soft and iron hard and she couldn't get enough of him. She pumped her hand to match the movement of her mouth, intoxicated by the scent of him and the taste of salt, the heat of the sun beating down on her back. His breathing was as laboured as hers now so she used both hands, her tongue, and increased her speed and suction.

'Kelsi,' he gasped. 'If you want what I think you want then you have to stop.' His fingers dug into her arms. 'Now.'

Flushed, she lifted her head and looked up at him. She firmed her grip on him and spoke her mind. 'I don't want to stop.' She wanted him to come hard and loud and utterly uncontrollably—as she had.

He closed his eyes. Flashed them open again, determination anew in his expression. He moved fast. Pulling the straps of her bra down, and then the cups, so her breasts were in his hands.

'Beautiful.' He strained up, gusting hot air on her nipple just before he sucked it into his mouth.

She shook, her fingers loosening their grip on him. At that he moved, flipping her over onto the sand, the water splashing as he pressed kisses to her belly, his hands peeling her sodden knickers down.

He stopped as he looked at her exposed body, his eyes widening. 'You're a redhead.'

Kelsi screwed her eyes shut. She wasn't red. She wished she were—a lovely rich auburn or something. But in truth she was orange. As in carroty. Bright orange hair with almost see-through skin that freckled up the moment she got within ten miles of a sunny spot. She'd spent her childhood being teased about it—dyed it the minute she'd had the money to buy the chemicals. Thank goodness for L'Oreal.

But she was still orange down there, although she'd thought about dying that many times, too. Sensitive skin meant she'd never taken the risk. Her self-consciousness sprang back as the joy got killed. She moved, wanting to curl away so he could no longer see her. Years of taunts haunted her. The reaction was never good from men. She should have remembered that. But he moved, his hands gripping her, his leg weighing heavy on hers so she couldn't escape. And he looked up at her, his blue eyes seeming to pierce right through her.

'Don't tell me you were going to get rid of it at the spa today.' He slid a finger through the narrow strip of hair and suddenly she lost the ability to even think about moving away. 'It's beautiful.' He stroked her some more before bending down and licking her as slowly and with as much reverence as a man knowing it was his last ever taste of paradise. 'Don't ever get rid of it.'

It was the first time a man had even hinted that he liked it. The few others she'd been with had seemed to find it amusing—and not in a way that made her feel very sexy.

Jack looked up at her, registering how still she was. 'I mean it.' And then he bent again, his mouth convincing her wordlessly.

Her legs parted wider with his touch, her desire sky-rocketing again—only more so. Never had she felt so desired. Never had she had someone hold her like this.

'Jack.'

'Yeah.' He twisted, grabbing the shorts that were half-way down to his ankles. He pulled them off, pulled his wallet from the pocket, pulled a condom from that. She was glad he'd thought of contraception because it hadn't even occurred to her in the madness that was this lust. In moments he'd rolled it on and was back beside her, his hand heavy and low on her stomach.

'I wanted this the second I saw you,' he said bluntly. 'Was it the same for you?'

In this majestic setting there could only be truth. 'Of course.' She ran her fingers down his jaw, her thumb across his lower lip. 'You're incredibly handsome.'

'And you're bewitching.'

Her body reacted swiftly to the compliment—her nipples going even harder, her inner thighs tightening in anticipation. She smiled, fluttered her lashes as she peeped up at him. 'A witch now? No longer a vampire?'

He tilted his head on the side and seemed to assess

her slowly, the smile on his lips widening. 'I'm thinking nymph.'

'Oh-h-h.' Her juices flowed faster. 'A nymph.'

She arched her hips against him, her intent pure provocation—a playfulness that was so new, and yet so much fun. 'You think?'

'A very sexy nymph.' He lifted his hand to cup her face. 'A nymph I'm going to have to have.'

'Then hurry up and have me.'

The sand was warm and wet on her back, but his body above hers was even hotter. He frowned slightly as he braced above her. 'You're tiny.'

Oh. That had been a past complaint, too. Why did she even bother with a bra when there was barely anything to bounce.

'I don't want to crush you.' His voice choked.

Oh. He didn't just mean her breasts? She glanced down his body. He was a lot bigger than her. But she wasn't a china doll. 'You won't.'

But he was careful as he settled his weight on her—too careful. She arched again, rocking her hips, teasing him. He was close enough now for her to slide her slick sex back and forth against the hard head of his. His jaw firmed as she did it again and again. She didn't want gentle. She wanted wild and crazy. And she wanted it now.

His large hand gripped her hip, stopping her. Their eyes locked and then in one powerful motion he moved into her. A sure, strong stroke. She cried out as he filled her.

'Too much?' he rasped.

'More,' she pleaded, almost insane with the sensation. 'Please more.'

He paused but then pushed forward again.

She shuddered, the pleasure so exquisite that she couldn't cope, crying out as he drove her deeper and then deeper into the blissful abyss. She gasped, sucking in a lungful of sea air as she struggled to stay together. And a couple more deep gasps later she got it—her rhythm, her strength. Able to meet him stroke for stroke, she half moaned, half laughed and traced her hands over him, glorying in the incredible body riding hers.

Oh, sweet mercy, the man was fit. And as their movements merged into the one perfectly matched rhythm he flipped them both, holding her fast to him until she was astride and he beneath. The water splashed around them, but did nothing to cool.

She looked down at him and teased. 'I don't want to crush you.'

His grin flashed, too. But then she reached behind her, down to where their bodies met, and, cupping his balls in her hand, she squeezed ever so slightly.

His harsh groan ricocheted through her as he quaked. His hands gripped her tighter and he sat up, changing the angle in a way that made her draw a quick, delicious breath.

'You're in for it now, honey.' His hair dripped salt water, his smile gleamed wickedly.

Their slick chests sealed as he held her in his large hands, rocking her onto him, around him. Until she was panting and pleading—but he didn't let her have the release then. No, he merely moved once more—moved her—and began the torture all over again.

They were naked under the searing sun, in the lapping water. Instruments of pleasure—mindless, endless pleasure. There was no past, no future, no innocence or experience. Nothing but the two of them and the magic that flared in the marathon moment. The freedom was intoxicating—a wild, reckless feeling that had her wanting all kinds of things, here and now and deeply physical.

Blind touch, pure sensation, wild eroticism.

And ecstasy.

Screaming, raw ecstasy.

Kelsi let her eyelids open just a fraction so some of the brilliant blue sky above her was visible. She felt their heartbeats galloping, the water washing over them higher and higher as the waves rose and fell. She was completely naked beneath a near stranger on a barren bay. It was beautiful.

'Thank you,' she murmured.

She felt him take in a deep breath, felt him relax that bit more as he exhaled and answered. 'It was such a pleasure.' He lifted up onto one hand, a slightly rueful look in his eye. 'I wanted this place to seduce you,' he admitted. '*I* wanted to seduce you.'

'And I feel so much better for it.'

He smiled.

The ebb and flow of the waves, the sound in her ears made her even happier. 'It's such a cliché.' She giggled.

'It's a universal truth. Fresh air always clears your head.'

Fresh air and a hunk of a man to fulfil every sensual wish.

'But you need to get out of the sun,' he said, running a finger over her shoulder before slipping away, splashing back into the water.

He dived, swimming out—for a moment looking like some fantasy merman or something. Except he had legs. Really good, muscular ones.

She sighed, reluctant to move, but then if she didn't she really was going to drown. She sat up and looked about for her clothes. Her most expensive lingerie was floating back and forth on the tide, ruined by sand and salt water.

She screwed it into a ball and put it in the drenched hat with the equally sodden wrap. Thankfully her dress had landed farther up on the beach and remained largely dry. Most of the sand tumbled from the fabric as she shook it, but there was still half the beach in her hair and sticking to her body. She didn't care. She really didn't care—still on a high from the most intense sensual experience of her life.

She turned to watch him emerge from the water. The faint imprint in the sand that their bodies had made as they'd lain together was just visible. But as she watched the waves washed the marks away. Just like that, it was a smooth blank canvas once more. They might never have been there. No one ever would know. But she didn't want the memory to go just like that. She wanted to savour it like the precious thing it was.

She slipped into her dress and tried not to watch too obviously as he pulled on his shorts. He really did have the most incredible body she'd ever seen.

'So.' She cleared her throat. 'Training in Canada?' It wasn't that the silence was awkward, but she needed to think of something normal and stop the spinning of her nerves.

'Yeah, I've been in the pool a lot to keep my fitness up, but there I'll get back on the slopes.' He matched her steps as she walked back along the beach, eventually turning up towards the car. From the corner of her eye she could see his mostly bare, bronzed body.

Deep inside she softened again while her breasts tightened. Muscles that had been languid were licked to attention by anticipation once more as she remembered the moments that had passed too soon. She knew that when they got back to the car the spell would be broken—but she wanted to feel the magic some more. She wanted him again—this second.

Now that really was insane. She swallowed, trying to get a grip on her pulse as they walked beneath the stand of trees where her car was parked. But it was all she could think of—she wanted him to kiss her again, she wanted him to do everything again. Dear heaven, she wanted to do it all and more to him. The crazy lust overwhelmed her again. She stumbled. His hand shot out and he grabbed her wrist, helping her regain her balance.

'Kelsi?' He pulled, gently drawing her close to him.

She stared up at him, overwhelmed by the chaos of emotions running through her body. She'd never had a sensual experience like that before. She'd never felt revered or wanted or as desirable as that. She'd never felt as at one with another—so in sync, so comfortable. She'd never come with a man like that before.

And she was so grateful she was near to tears.

Jack lifted her up so he could kiss her again. Pushing down the growl of frustration that threatened to emerge from his mouth as if he were some bear just out of hibernation and lethally hungry. He was shaking with starvation now—but they couldn't do it again.

Damn.

She trembled as he put her on the bonnet of her car; he felt the answering spasm in his muscles and clutched her even closer.

'I only had the one condom.' He groaned, forcing himself to cling to reality. 'Kids aren't part of my plan.'

'No,' she muttered.

'We have to stop.'

'Mmm…' Her hands skated across his chest.

He grabbed them between his, holding them firm. 'Not helping, Kelsi.'

But he couldn't not kiss her. Not when she looked as disappointed as he felt. He liked ultraphysical sex—pushing it hard. Full-on and frantic, leaving him and his lover both too exhausted to move. Like everything he did, he liked it to extremes. He'd thought the beach had been his most extreme experience ever. He'd thought he wouldn't be able to get hard again for at least twelve hours. But here he was filled and ready to fire not much more than fifteen minutes later.

He swore hard in his head while his mouth ravaged hers. Burning up for this surprisingly fit woman who seemed to still be as hungry as he—who'd just given him the most sensational sex of his life. But he made himself ease it back, slow it down so their kisses soothed rather than stirred.

Yet even those gentle touches were an indulgence he couldn't give up. Not when she nipped and then suckled on his lower lip like that, not when her small fingers tugged at his hair so he'd bring his head closer again.

Yeah, kissing her was irresistible. And the idea of being inside her again became imperative. He could take her back to his hotel and they could spend the night together. She made him feel invincible, filled with unending energy. Raw sexual attraction—and a compatibility that astounded him given their physical disparity.

She had colour now—pretty pink rose petals bloomed in her cheeks. So much nicer than the pallor when she'd come flying out of the car to see if she'd killed him. The fresh air suited her; so did the kissed senseless look.

But when he lifted his head to look at her beautiful body, he realised the light was darkening. He looked to the sky—heavy clouds had rolled across and were dropping lower with every second. Canterbury was famed for providing four seasons in one day and it seemed the weather had gone from summer to winter in minutes. The wind lifted, no longer the crazy warm breeze but a cold, threatening blast. And despite the way he ran his hands over her, he could see the goose bumps peppering her upper arms. They had to go. But he didn't want to destroy this moment.

'We need to get back to town,' he said, sounding harsh with frustration. 'It's going to rain.'

The disappointment darkened her eyes even more and he saw then just how tired she was. So he kissed her again, his hands gently rubbing her upper arms, slowly and lightly. Then he told her, 'I'm driving back.'

He saw her hesitation, just knew she was going to argue, so he kissed her again until she was lax and he could feel her soft drowsiness. He repeated his intention and smiled as she muttered OK.

Ten minutes into the drive she'd twisted sideways in the seat and gone to sleep—smiling. She looked so sweet. So vulnerable. And so not his type. Jack looked back to the road as he felt the big fat *oops* hit him.

Despite her sophisticated surface there was a sensitive depth there. He'd seen it in her terror after the accident, he'd just forgotten it when she'd turned sex kitten on him on the sand. And frankly he'd been too hot for her to be able to stop anyway. He'd wanted, and he'd got—just like always.

But she was a softy, wasn't she? And that soft side was only going to get scrunched if she hung out with him any more than another five minutes. He liked fun with women who were as strong as he—who could handle physical challenge without emotional entanglements. She'd hardly been able to handle a near-miss car prang. Hell, she'd probably still been in shock after the accident and he'd just taken total advantage of her. He felt really bad now. He couldn't spend the rest of the day fulfilling carnal fantasies with her—even if it was what his body was screaming at him to do. He really didn't want to hurt her and he'd seen the vulnerability in her eyes—he'd seen her surprise when he'd shown his interest. She wasn't a player.

So it was better to end it all now.

As he waited at a red light on the city side of the hill he leaned across and woke her with an irresistible last little kiss. 'Where do you live?'

She stirred, blinking rapidly as she told him. He drove straight there, determined to finish up this oh-so-gorgeous interlude before he was tempted back to touch more.

'You don't want me to drop you somewhere?' She straightened up in her seat.

He shook his head. 'The walk will be good for my knee.'

If she went within a mile radius of his hotel he'd drag her in with him.

He pulled over where she'd said to. 'Big house.'

Her pretty nose wrinkled. 'It's been converted into four flats. It's all carved up inside.'

He looked closer at the old stately house. One of the last original buildings remaining on the street—and the For Sale sign up in front of it meant she'd probably be moving soon. The property would be demolished and developers would put up ten town houses in its place—as what had happened with the rest of the street. Shame for the old dame—despite the wear and lack of love the structure was solid and the detail handcrafted.

He got out of her car, trying to ignore the horrible tightening inside. He didn't much like drawn-out goodbyes. But she moved so she was right in front of him, standing on her tiptoes in her bare feet, her fingers lightly cupping his jaw so she ensured she had his attention.

'You were right, you know,' she said simply. 'Thanks so much, Jack.'

He swallowed and nodded and simply couldn't give her a kiss. Oddly hurt that she so readily accepted that there wasn't going to be anything more between them. Not really wanting to be thanked as if it were some kind of service he'd provided—as if he'd just been her intimate masseuse or something.

Hell, maybe she was tougher than she looked. Maybe he should just go in there with her and explore the comfort of her bed. Except she was walking. Away. As if she didn't care at all—and that was for the best, right?

'Good luck with your training,' she called.

He stood on the footpath and watched her open the big wooden door. Not moving until it had closed again behind her—because he was too tempted to storm in there after her and kiss her 'til she begged him to be inside her again. But she'd disappeared now, so he walked, trying to make his tense muscles relax—reminding himself that he'd just had a fun time on a beach with a cute girl. That was all. Nothing more. Nothing serious.

But he couldn't shake the uneasy feeling that he'd just left a part of himself behind.

CHAPTER FOUR

THERE was always a pin to burst a bubble. And it didn't take long for Kelsi to find one. All she'd had to do was enter 'Jack' and 'professional snowboarder' and 'New Zealand' into her computer.

Jack Greene was featured on a zillion webpages. And no wonder he looked as if he'd stepped out of a catalogue—he really had, modelling for the snow'n'skate chain of stores he'd got her the hat and wrap from. For their exclusive New Zealand designed snowboard gear range—he was the celebrity endorsement.

Worse still, he was Jack Greene of the Pure Greene Trust that owned Karearea—the Maori name for the New Zealand falcon—and a private ski field. A couple of hours' drive from Christchurch, it was the favourite winter playground of New Zealand's sporting elite and showbiz celebrities and snobby super-rich people. Home to the exclusive, green-powered, luxury lodge where visiting Hollywood actors stayed when they were on a break from their location shoots and wanted to soak up the splendour of the Southern Alps. Kelsi's jaw dropped as she went on the virtual tour of it on the website. The man was loaded.

Then there were the video clips—and they totally diverted her. She watched some, barely peeping between her fingers as he defied gravity, reality and plain common sense by jumping off sheer edges of mountains, spinning round thirty times mid-air and then landing on the snow upright and coasting fast on a board that surely should have broken. *He* should have broken—and would have if he'd misjudged by even a millimetre.

And then there were the women. He had no less than five different fan pages on Facebook—featuring the modelling pictures from years ago, the stills taken when he was midair in some jump. People tweeted with sightings of him and had pictures of them smiling standing next to him by the T-bar or chairlift.

She'd had no idea there was such a scene with snowboarding. As rock stars had their groupies, snowboarders seemed to have their bunnies—beautiful women who were all long limbs and athletically capable. Some of them did those hair-raising jumps, too, some of them wore *bikinis* on the slopes—and all of them were clearly willing to do whatever with him.

So why on *earth* had Jack Greene ever bothered with her?

He must have been bored and caught by an impulse. Entertaining himself for a few hours before a mind-numbing plane ride. It was the only explanation. She cringed—it must have been so average for him. And she was so glad she'd managed a cool and sophisticated goodbye. Even though on the inside she'd been hoping he'd ask to spend the rest of the afternoon with her.

She'd never had such spontaneous, sensual sex. Never outdoors. Never a one-night—or mid-morning—stand. Sex had always been under the covers in the dark in one of her total of two relationships. Never so wild and free and reckless. Frankly, there was a lot to be said for it. But she'd never admit it to anyone—especially not now she knew she was one of a zillion to be slayed by him.

Next morning, heavy-hearted and unwilling to crawl out from hiding under her covers, she tried to tell herself it had all been a dream. If it weren't for the few marks on her body, the sweet aches in her muscles, maybe she could convince herself totally. But there were those marks, those aches and that yearning feeling that just wouldn't go away.

More. She'd always wanted more—from life, from lovers, most of all from herself. She sighed and flung back the covers. How was she going to be able to look her workmates in the eyes? How did she tell them she hadn't made it to that wretched appointment?

'Wow, you look amazing,' said Tom, who was on the other side of her partition in the office. 'You're glowing.'

Um, well, that would be the slight all-over-body sunburn. But she'd covered up in a filmy black ensemble that clung from her neck down.

'What treatments did you go for?' Tom was still staring.

Kelsi flushed and mumbled, 'A new sort of sand scrub.'

'Sand? Like from the Dead Sea or something?'

'Something like that.' Lying by omission wasn't as bad as a complete fabrication, was it?

'Awesome.' Tom's brows were almost to his hairline. 'I'm going to have to book my girlfriend in for one of those. It's done wonders for you.' He stepped closer and looked at Kelsi's eyes. 'What colour?'

'Rose.' She badly needed that tint on the world today.

She got her moisturiser from her drawer and smoothed it over her hands as she read through her emails. Then she forced her brain to concentrate on work. But she kept slipping. She'd been played so beautifully. Maybe falling for womanisers was a genetic thing because her mum had made that mistake, too. Kelsi's own dad had been the local

Lothario. Impossible as she found it to believe. But the red in his hair was more strawberry blonde, his skin tanned more easily, making his eyes less weird and more attractive. But he'd been so charming, so full of it. Her mother had forgiven him, taken him back three times before he left for good. That time he'd found another woman to make the perfect family with. She'd had the pretty daughter that his blood daughter wasn't ever going to be. And Kelsi had been sucked in, too—believed his lines only to be let down too many times.

But her dad wasn't anywhere near the level of Jack Greene. Jack was a conqueror—now she knew. She wasn't surprised either. She'd guessed he had success and experience with women. And she bet that once he'd conquered, he moved on to new challenges—a.s.a.p. That was the kind of adrenaline-fuelled lifestyle he'd lead.

And that was OK. She didn't hold it against him. It wasn't as if he'd made her any promises. He hadn't lied and pretended there'd be anything more to them—in fact, he'd been careful to make sure she understood.

But of course he'd known just how to look at her, how to hold her to make her feel so special—so that saying no was an impossibility. He was a master of passion. The ultimate playboy. While that didn't mean she couldn't still enjoy the memory, she'd probably be better off if she just forgot about it. It hadn't been that special at all—certainly not for him.

But no matter how many times she vacuumed her car she couldn't get all the sand out. In the end she handed over the money for a professional full-service valet. The car came back smelling of chemicals strong enough to burn her nostrils. But it was better than the hint of sun and surf and sex that had lingered for days. Every time she got into the damn thing she saw a mirage of him—his broad shoulders leaning across with his head in her lap as he'd removed her shoe. Yeah, in her mind she saw his head in her lap way too often.

Maybe she'd discovered her penchant for anonymous mid-morning stands. Maybe she should try for another. But the idea of any other man repulsed her. None looked even remotely attractive—none could compare. She couldn't shake him from her head. She dreamed of him, she thought she saw him in the distance on the street. And she sat in the office and stared out at the hills way too much. Stupid to imagine herself back out there—she'd much rather be indoors looking at beautiful art and design.

Trouble was, Jack Greene had the most beautifully designed body she'd ever seen. Memories flooded her and she struggled to keep on top of them—and on her body's continual slow burn. So she worked even harder than usual, taking on several more projects. Working so hard and so long that by the end of each day she was so exhausted she slept—at least for some of the night.

Weeks later, even more swamped and exhausted by her workload, she parked her car outside her flat. The old house still hadn't sold, and she was glad, despite being the only tenant left in the big building. She locked the car and went to find a packet of instant food.

But someone was sitting on the deck. Her footsteps slowed as she walked nearer. Not sure she could trust her eyes. She knew that hair, that face, most definitely that body. He'd been in her dreams for the last month.

She couldn't believe he was here. Or that he was wearing jeans and shirt quite like that. She remembered the strength in those thighs. The tight butt. Not to mention the hard, flat abs, the broad chest and the sleek curves of his shoulders as he'd arched above her. No fat, just long, lean muscle and smooth burnished skin. And the smattering of hair that arrowed to…

Yes. She stood transfixed at the bottom of the steps—because she knew that beneath the designer casual and the fancy watch the raw body was even better.

'Hey, Kelsi.' With his athletic grace he rose to his feet and smiled.

'Jack,' she swallowed. 'This is a surprise.'

'Yeah,' he agreed. 'I wanted to see you.'

Why? All kinds of crazy reasons raced through her brain but none of the good options could be possible. It had to be bad, or maybe he was just passing and stopped to say hi or something. It couldn't be that she'd made any kind of impact on him.

She didn't have the courage to ask, didn't have the courage to look into those blinding eyes again because one of the best things about her time with Jack was that it had been rejection-free—so she didn't want to ask for it now. She settled on a safe question instead. 'You want to come in for a coffee or something?'

A self-serving invite anyway. Coffee would clear her head—wake her up enough to work out whether this was just one of those hot dreams or not.

'Thanks.'

Jack couldn't wrench his gaze from her as he followed her up the stairs. Some sort of skull cap covered most of her hair, only a few blonde tufts appeared around the edges. Her face was as pale as ever but her eyes were really something—silver irises—almost as reflective as a mirror. They went perfectly with the shimmering silver dress that hung as the top layer over the black fabric swamping every inch of her skin. She looked like an ethereal nymph of the night. And she turned him on to an almost uncontrollable degree. He wanted to push the shiny thin fabric to the ground so he could see the perfect, petite treasure beneath. He wanted to slide the contacts from her eyes so he could see the true colour she so determinedly hid—and her true expression. Her entire outfit was a cover. So was her cool response to him now—or so he hoped anyway, because she hadn't exactly been all immediate warmth and touch like the occasional reunions he'd had with other lovers. But then Kelsi wasn't anything like those other lovers, was she? That was the problem—she was the only one to haunt him.

He watched her unlock her door. He could see the acceleration of her breathing, the faint colour deepening in her cheeks and he felt his own response deepen—horrific in its intensity. For weeks now all he'd been able to think about was the heat of her on that mad day by the beach. The sweetness, the wildness, the total sexiness.

It was a nightmare distraction. He needed his focus back—because his training was a mess. But it was an attitude problem, not his knee. He had to clear his head and to do that he needed to get Kelsi out of it. Never had a woman interfered with his goals before. Never had he allowed another person to influence his schedule the way Kelsi had. Not that she knew it—or was going to know it. No, this was all about him getting rid of the fantasy for good because he was furious with himself for being this pathetic. He had not got as far as he had by letting personal needs or wants get in the way of competition prep—he wasn't going to derail now. That gold medal was going to be his.

He just hoped this would do it. He'd see her again and realise it hadn't been that spectacular—that memory had somehow magnified how amazing they'd been together. But now he was here and now it was worse—all he wanted was to have her again, to know her, to make her laugh. She was every bit as cute as he remembered, every bit as crazy, every bit as breathtaking. She had the towering platform shoes on again that were probably killing her toes with narrowness and still he was burning up worse than a meteor in the atmosphere.

But he forced the rampaging lust down, needing to check her reaction some more. She was reserved and not looking him in the eyes and keeping her distance. A new thing for him.

Still, what had he expected? He hadn't, of course—he'd been indulging in the wicked side of fantasy, not the realistic. To buy time he stared around her little flat. There was a lot to take in—it was completely crammed with stuff. Books were a main feature, all lined up along a wall. He skimmed the spines. Many he'd read but he didn't keep them as she did. He passed them on, left them somewhere. But Kelsi was definitely a 'keeper' kind of person. Every inch of her apartment was filled—reflecting eclectic tastes and a very busy mind. There was enough confusion to cause a headache. The walls closed in on him—he didn't keep 'things', he liked to travel so he could move fast and free.

He blinked at the visual cacophony, but slowly began to see some order in the chaos. Things weren't tossed wherever, they were placed. And there was also the completely crazy. Like the Lilliputian-sized curling staircase in one corner of the lounge leading up to—the wall. Painted on the wall was not a doorway, as you'd expect, but a Japanese fan spread open.

'Why?' He pointed at it and looked at her.

She glanced at the mini-stairs. 'Why not?'

OK, he grinned. He should have known. And, oh, man, her coolness was a temptation. He turned away from her, needing to get distracted again, else he'd just haul her to him caveman style and he really wanted to know he could be more controlled than a caveman. And her lack of super-obvious signals maybe meant she had some regrets. He hoped not—all he regretted was that he'd left. He should have taken her to his hotel until he'd blown her from his system completely.

So now he stopped by the wall where there was a giant picture frame hanging. A huge gilt number—it would be the focal point if he were sitting on the sofa. But it was empty—not even a blank canvas inside it, just the bare white wall. 'Tell me about this.'

'Watch.' She flicked a switch and an image suddenly appeared in the frame.

He looked up—clamped to the ceiling was an old slide projector. He looked back to the frame and watched as she clicked through a series of slides—mostly modern paintings. Frankly weird ones.

'You studied art,' he said.

'Art history, yes.'

'But you did some yourself?'

She frowned. 'Not formally, no. But I like to play around.' She clicked through another couple of eyesore slides.

'You don't have any landscapes?' he couldn't help asking.

'What, like mountain scenes?'

'Yeah.' He grinned.

'No,' she said flatly and put the remote down.

He chuckled and wandered around the room. On the table was a single flower—some big, beautiful bloom that looked delicate, as if the petals would fall if you so much as brushed it. Yet she'd put it in an antique glass bottle that had a worn 'poison' sticker on it. He grinned at the juxtaposition. He looked again at the stairway to nowhere, the paintings, the vases, the collection of kitsch knick-knacks overflowing on one shelf while the shelf beside that one was completely bare. 'You have a lot of weird things.'

'Things that don't readily make sense,' she agreed. 'It's a way of freeing up my imagination. To encourage creativity.'

OK—by having a collection of plastic animals walking up the wall? He lifted his brow at the rhino that had a miniature bottle opener hanging from its horn.

'Mystery is always present,' she said softly. 'That's the point.'

He looked at her. Yeah, the mystery was right in front of him. Adrenaline rushed, the precursor to fight, to drive for success. In that instant he wanted her more than he wanted his next breath.

Jack was staring at her. Just staring. Making her feel so self-conscious and so hot it was a wonder her skin wasn't curling and crisping like bacon under a grill.

'What are you doing here?' she asked before thinking.

'I'm deciding whether you're real or whether this is jet lag causing a hallucination.'

Jet lag? Had he only just got back from Canada?

'How are you going to find out?' She could barely breathe.

He smiled lazily and she blinked in the face of its brilliance. Oh, he was so smooth, wasn't he? She couldn't be felled again by just a look like that.

She leaned forward—dangerously close. 'I'm an illusion,' she whispered. 'Not real at all.'

He chuckled.

'How was your trip?' She stepped back and busied her hands by going into the kitchen and getting cups from the shelf. 'Did the training go OK?'

'Not as good as it could have.' He followed her, leaning against the door frame.

'No?'

His grimace said it all. 'My knee is going to take a little longer than we first thought. I'm back for more physio. No point getting frustrated by being surrounded by snow and doing something stupid.'

'Oh.' She'd thought he'd handled the stairs no problem and was moving as lithe as a panther. But it must still bother him on those death-defying jumps.

'What about you—you're OK?' He moved to where she was by the bench. Mind-blowingly, pheromone-dizzying close.

She stared at the seam of his shirt and reminded herself to breathe again. She had to keep it light. Didn't want him to know how much he affected her—that was just embarrassing. The guy was a pro—but in sport and sex. And she was just another in that long line. So she had to get them laughing again as if none of this had ever mattered.

'Actually, no,' she said firmly. 'Life's not been the same since I last saw you.'

He stilled. 'It hasn't?'

'No,' she said sombrely. 'Thanks to you I'm scarred for life.' With a theatrical flourish, she pointed to her nose. 'I got three new freckles.'

'Freckles,' he said blankly. 'You got freckles.'

'Three.' She nodded. 'From the sun.'

He snorted and leaned back on the bench, his smile crocodile wide.

She grinned back. 'You obviously aren't aware of how serious this is.'

He laughed—too long, too infectiously. Then he suddenly sobered, half groaning and rubbing his chest with the heel of his hand. 'Hell, for a moment there I thought you were going to tell me something far worse.'

'What could be worse?' she asked mock-incredulously.

'That there might have been some long-term consequences from that day.'

'Freckles are long term,' she said. 'You can't get rid of them. At *all*. Believe me, I've tried.'

'But kids have much more of an impact.' He shook his head and laughed again. 'I thought you were going to tell me you were pregnant.'

Pregnant?

Kelsi laughed, too—giggled like a silly schoolgirl.

But as their amusement filled her ears her brain ticked over slowly. Her giggle went into cardiac arrest.

'Kelsi?'

She shook her head and turned away from him slightly as she tried to think harder. Pregnant. No. She'd had a period—hadn't she?

'It's been a month, Kelsi. Shouldn't you know by now?'

She should if she'd been paying attention to anything like that. But she'd been working even crazier hours than usual because of an account she'd won. Because she'd been trying to distract herself so much.

So she really hadn't been thinking about her cycle or anything. Hell, she hadn't even had the time to dye her hair again, which was why she was going for the assortment of hats at the moment.

'Kelsi?'

Stupid, irrelevant thoughts tumbled over and over in her head. When had her last period been? But all she came up with was an empty feeling. A blankness that just couldn't be good.

'I used a condom.' Clearly he was thinking the same thing.

'Yes.' Her voice cracked. 'You checked it after, right?'

He stared at her but wasn't really seeing her. She knew he, too, was thinking back on those cataclysmic moments when they'd been in the water. Waist deep, they'd rolled and swapped positions again and again and pushed it every which way.

His face became more rigid as the seconds dragged. 'I swam after. I just scrunched it up and put it in my pocket to get rid of later.'

So he hadn't checked—it could have shredded. Neither of them knew for sure. And, given the sustained action the thing had endured, it probably had.

Oh, no.

'Come on,' He said suddenly, taking her hand in a tight grip and next thing he was walking her out of the flat, down the path, dragging her behind him like one of those wooden pull-along toys.

He went to the driver's side of her car. 'Keys.'

'I thought you believed in *walking*,' she said sarcastically, needing to get a bite in.

'Right now I really feel like running.'

Ha ha.

She got in the car and gripped her hands tight together, pressing them to her chest. 'Where are we going?'

'The supermarket.'

She looked blankly at him.

'To get a pregnancy test.'

Supermarkets stocked pregnancy tests? And he knew this how?

'They have everything. If they don't we'll try the pharmacy.'

But the supermarket did have pregnancy tests—next to the lubricant and the ribbed condoms.

'I can't do this.' She dropped her gaze down to the plasters—brightly coloured ones with cartoon characters on them. She looked to another shelf—kids' toothpaste, kids' shampoo, kids' talc. Everywhere she looked there were kid things. Only a little farther along were nappies—*nappies!*

No, no, no and no again.

Jack didn't answer, just reached up and grabbed two boxes—different brands. Then he took her by the arm again and stalked to another aisle, picked up a bottle of juice.

'I prefer apple,' she said, just to retain some element of control.

'There must be a bathroom somewhere round here.' He looked around the building.

'I am not doing this in a public loo.' She shook her head, appalled. 'I'm going home.'

He frowned but nodded. 'I'm coming with you.'

She saw the look in his eyes and decided not to argue. She went ahead so she wouldn't have to see the checkout operator's eyebrows lift when she scanned those few specific items.

He got in the car and handed her the bottle. She held it in a death grip but she couldn't drink. She didn't want to move—not even an inch, not ever again. The bottle was taken from her and he took a gulp from it. She'd laugh if she wasn't so scared. He was on her heels as she walked up the path to her building. She could feel his breath on her shoulder as she unlocked the door. But when he walked with her up to the bathroom door she drew the line.

'I'm having privacy for this.'

'Of course. I'll be right here.' He handed her the plastic shopping bag, then took up position leaning against the wall right outside.

This just couldn't be happening. Just couldn't.

She'd never done a pregnancy test in her life, but it wasn't as if it was hard. Hideous, yes, as her stomach swirled with sickened nerves. She held the little stick thing in front of her and watched as she waited to see if her life really was ruined. She'd opened the most expensive one first, hoping it meant greatest accuracy, but all it meant was that it was the one that flashed the result in a bright neon light—*pregnant!*

As if it were the best news in all the world.

For some women it would be. For some women it would be the result they'd been praying for after months of trying or treatment. But for Kelsi?

She slumped. An unplanned pregnancy was bad enough. But from a one-night stand? Not even a relationship? They had no basis, nothing to try to make the best of, nothing between them but animal, sexual attraction—that was as everyday to him as breathing. And utterly overwhelming for her.

Wincing, she closed her eyes. But still she saw the light flashing with that single, life-changing word.

It had to be wrong. Had to be.

She ripped open the second box.

CHAPTER FIVE

JACK banged on the door, never so impatient in all his life. 'Kelsi? Are you okay? Open up.'

Silence. Just as there'd been silence for the last ten interminable minutes.

'If you don't open up now I'm breaking the door.'

It wouldn't take much. He seemed to have more adrenaline running in him than he'd had even on the most difficult jumps. He made himself uncurl his fingers from the fists they'd bunched into and tried to relax. Half a second later he banged again.

There was a muffled reply. Not good.

The door opened and he saw her face.

Definitely not good. Definitely really, really bad.

'Don't worry.' He didn't know who he was trying to reassure more—her or him. 'It's going to be OK.'

Oh, hell, it wasn't. She walked past him, handed him the thing that had 'pregnant' flashing on the tip—two of them plus two that had the two blue lines. He'd seen enough movies to know what they all meant; he didn't need the damn flashing neon signs.

Was this why he hadn't been able to get her out of his head these past weeks? Was there such a thing as male intuition?

No. It was pure lust. All day, all night she was all he

could think about, until he could fight it no more and he'd
had to come and deal with it. He'd actually blown off his
training and come back to finish what they'd started. That
was nightmare enough, now it had turned into a full-on
horror film.

His brain fast-tracked down another nightmare route.
Had she known? She'd been cool when she first saw him—
had she known she was pregnant but was never going to
tell him? Would she *ever* have told him?

He stared at her. Of course she hadn't known. No one
could fake this kind of shocked reaction. But would she
have told him once she found out? The question burned
deep and he didn't like it.

'We can deal with this,' he said into the silence, still
trying to reassure someone—anyone.

She said nothing. Just looked stricken.

Problem solving. He could do that. He just had to
figure out a plan. But he wasn't thinking much at all at
the moment other than—*pregnant.*

And then came the panic. The sheer, freezing panic as
he thought about a baby and its birth and then about his
own awful arrival into the world.

'It is mine, right?' his mouth blabbed before his brain
could stop it.

She went rigid. 'Right.'

Big mistake. But he had to be sure—because there
were things she had to know. But not now—she was upset
enough already. She didn't need more to terrify her. Oh,
hell, no.

'I take full responsibility,' he said urgently. 'I was the
one who—'

'I said yes,' she interrupted fiercely. 'I don't blame
you.'

Silence. Long, long silence. But doubts whispered inside

and he, who usually had such formidable mental strength, now could not resist them. 'Can I ask you something?'

She shrugged. 'Sure.'

'If I hadn't come here tonight, would you have contacted me when you found out? Would I ever have known I'm going to be a father?'

Kelsi didn't think the evening could have got worse. But it just had. 'We don't know each other very well, do we?' she said bleakly. 'Of course I would have.'

She turned away from him and walked to the window. What a mess. But this was one she had to get control of really quickly. And freeing Jack was right up there on her priority list. Because he was a Jack-the-lad all the way. He lived for adrenaline and extreme sports and travelling the globe year round and he needed it like that. He wasn't up for this, and she wasn't up for him being trapped and resentful. Or for her having her self-respect decimated as her mum's had been. Kelsi didn't want someone who played so fast and loose wandering in and out of her life. Or her child's. She didn't want her baby disappointed every time its daddy didn't turn up. And on top of that, his questioning if the baby was his hurt—he might play like that, she didn't.

She flung back her head. 'You know what? I'm not ashamed about what we did on the beach. I'm not going to be ever. I enjoyed it—you already know that. But it's irrelevant. This is going to take some time to get used to.' She swallowed. 'I just want to think and decide what to do.' She wanted him to go away and leave her free to do just that.

'Do I get to have any say what that decision might be?'

She looked up at him again. 'No.' His gaze sharpened

but she held her ground. 'You don't know me. You don't know what decisions I might be contemplating.'

'Then I suggest we get to know each other.' He walked towards her. 'Fast.'

Kelsi stiffened at the aggression in his voice and body. He'd better not be going to get all he-man and decisive. He'd better not get all controlling and telling her what to do. And he'd sure as hell better not be planning on ruining what little of her life there was left to ruin by forcing them into some kind of relationship when he'd never intended one before.

'I'm not leaving, Kelsi.' He spoke quickly, sounding all action man and making her think that was exactly what he was going to do. 'I'm not ditching you in the face of disaster. I don't operate like that. But we can work it out. We can—'

'We're not getting married.' She cut him off before he could get out the crazy proposal. 'I'm not marrying you. It's not necessary. That sort of thing just doesn't happen now.'

His eyes were wide.

'You don't need to worry,' she added furiously. 'I don't have a father to come running after you with a shotgun. It's a stupid idea.'

He paused, seeming to take a minute to breathe. Kelsi needed to sit. She wished he'd leave so she could process this whole thing; his presence was too much to cope with. She really wanted to cry—alone.

'Kelsi,' he said quietly. 'I don't want to get married either. I've no intention of ever getting married.'

Kelsi went prickly hot all over. He didn't? Oh, could the floor open up and swallow her now—*please?*

'You're right.' His voice softened further still. 'People don't marry because of unplanned pregnancies any more.'

While she totally agreed, somehow *him* saying it made her angry. His brutal honesty hurt. 'Some people don't go through with unplanned pregnancies either.'

The sharp intake of breath and the leaping in his eyes almost made her take a step back. 'I don't want this right now,' she said harshly. 'I have a career to build, I need to work—'

'You don't need to worry about money,' he said furiously. 'I will support you and the child.'

'No.' Her shoulders slumped. 'You don't need to. You don't need to worry. Just forget about it.' She didn't want him thinking he had to do anything.

He was white around the lips. 'You're going to get rid of it.'

She closed her eyes, holding back the tears. 'No,' she said softly. 'I'm sorry but that's not an option for me.'

She was the result of an unplanned pregnancy herself, the offspring of a shotgun wedding. So she knew all too well how those kinds of marriages failed. But she was grateful for her life. It wasn't this child's fault. She would love this child no matter that its conception was unintended. She'd made the mistake, but she wouldn't let her child suffer for it.

He turned away from her, lifting his arm and rubbing the side of his neck. 'Don't be sorry,' he said eventually. 'I'm glad.'

It was long moments before Kelsi could breathe again.

'We'll work it out.' He faced her again.

She held up her hand. She just didn't want to hear the platitudes. '*We* don't have to do anything. *I* do.' She sighed. 'Let's not have this conversation tonight.'

'Kelsi,' he asked softly. 'Where's your mum?'

She winced. How on earth was she going to tell her? She'd tried so hard to be the success her mother had wanted her to be. She didn't want to let her down and she just had. She'd never been able to meet her father's standard in looks, but for her mother she'd ensured she met the requirements—a good girl, with good grades and good attitude and good prospects. Not some hedonistic fool who'd throw it all away with a lust-filled romp with a stranger on a beach. How could she admit that folly? She couldn't bear to lose her mother's approval, too. Not when it had been so hard won.

When Kelsi answered it was a barely audible whisper. 'I'm not talking to her about this yet.'

Jack felt really bad now. She looked so small, so vulnerable. So damned vulnerable. And he couldn't stop himself from reaching out. Just to comfort, just a little. But she flinched back from his touch and looked wildly angry with him.

'Don't.' She glared at him.

OK, fair enough. He wasn't feeling that Disney happy either right now. He was worried—about her—in more ways than he wanted to admit to her or to himself. 'You haven't had dinner.'

'I'm not hungry.'

Nor was he. But it gave him reason to stick around. 'I'll go get something. Be back in twenty. We can talk some more then.'

A little cool-down time would be good for them both. His knee twinged as he strode to the row of shops down the end of the street but it wasn't as bad as the stabbing thoughts in his head. He'd never wanted to be responsible for anyone. He'd taken great care not to lead any lover on, or let anyone think themselves attached to him. He just wasn't ready for family commitments and he didn't think he'd ever be. He liked the thrill of variety and challenge—professionally and personally. He also liked to keep his distance from anything messy. That meant short, hot flings that ended in a nice friendship.

He liked his freedom. He needed it so he could concentrate on his career.

But there was something so galling about being told outright, from the outset, that he wasn't required. That any responsibility he felt wasn't necessary and nor was anything else he might want to offer. It annoyed him. And it made him Mr Contrary. For one crazy half-moment he'd even felt like insisting she marry him. Just to let her know she wasn't as self-sufficient as she thought. Because she wasn't. Sure, she had a job and car and everything, but she was renting and it wasn't as if she was rich. And he wasn't going to be easily sidelined.

But the truth was marriage hadn't even occurred to him until she'd pre-emptively refused him. Besides, he couldn't exactly force her.

Sanity prevailed. She was right, they didn't need to get married. He'd support their child—financially—of course he would. Hell, that was the one thing he could really offer. He knew how hard it had been for his father in the early years, trying to start up a business while caring for a baby on his own. Financial security had become his priority. At least Kelsi didn't have to worry about that. In that way Jack could give her a lot.

But, no, he wasn't going to be around full-time. His life just didn't work that way, but that didn't mean he should be ousted completely—which Kelsi obviously wanted. She was slicing the ground from beneath him. He really hadn't expected her to turn mother tiger on him and try to evict the male. In those minutes when he'd been waiting for the results he'd envisaged tearful scenes with her leaning on his shoulder, weak and helpless and needy. The reality of her rejection was far worse than the nightmare.

And then there was the brutal physical impact of pregnancy. He couldn't stop the worst-case scenario fears from spreading in his system like snake venom, threatening to shut down his vital organs, most especially his brain. Kelsi was petite—he remembered his hesitance on the beach when he worried he'd crush her—so the thought of her bearing the burden of his baby?

Terrifying.

His child could kill her. He knew. Because having him had killed his mother. Less than two hours after his birth, she'd gone.

He walked faster, trying to flee the fear and recover rational thought.

It wasn't going to happen. He wouldn't let it. Kelsi would have nothing but the best of medical care. His mother had had none. History would not repeat.

Twenty minutes later he was no less angry, no less determined, no less devastated as he walked back into Kelsi's flat with a couple of cartons of noodles. Neither of them touched them.

'It's going to be fine.' She smiled but it wasn't a natural one. 'It's all going to be OK.'

'Oh?' He stopped. She still had her back pressed against the window, as far away from him as possible.

'Sure.' She nodded. 'I have a good job. I have no worries financially. It won't be easy, but it'll be doable.'

Somehow that didn't make him feel any better. Now she was suggesting she didn't even want his money? Ridiculous. Doing it alone wasn't easy—even with only one child. His instincts sharpened—body becoming even more battle ready. 'What will you do with the baby?'

'When it comes I can keep working from home. Later I can return to the office part-time and work my hours back up as it gets older.'

'You've thought all this through,' he said, not keeping the sarcasm out.

She looked cool. 'Funnily enough, I haven't been able to think of much else.'

OK, so he knew it was the twenty-first century and all and there were plenty of working mothers out there, plenty of solo mothers, too, but there was that basic instinct in him now rearing its head up from the cave it had been born in, saying the man ought to provide for his woman and child. And there was another instinct rising, too, threatening to override everything—his need for this woman, pushing him to do what he'd been dreaming of for ever. 'And where did you see me fitting in with this?'

'I don't.'

'Pardon?' Jack couldn't control the snap of his muscles.

'I already said you don't need to worry about it.' Kelsi looked away from the wild expression in his eyes 'I can manage just fine on my own.' And she could. And she would.

'Really.' He looked furious. 'OK, let's say, for a second, that that's true.' He walked towards her, his anger surging ahead of him in an invisible cloud. 'Let's say you can manage just fine on your own and you don't *need* me.'

Kelsi froze, despite her instinct screaming at her to run. And then it was too late. He swiftly pulled her into his arms—lifting her right off her feet. Her heart thundered at the feel of his hard strength pressed so close to her. And it almost beat right out of her chest as his mouth descended.

Her whole body convulsed as his lips pressed hard on hers. It was anger she tasted, but also passion. And she couldn't do anything except put her hands around his neck and hold on. She tried so hard to stop the spinning inside but she couldn't contain her response, couldn't stop herself softening, opening for him and feeling the rush of desire for more. He was all strength, all heat. And all fury.

She shuddered deeply again as he ravaged, showing her no mercy, kissing her until she succumbed completely— not just to his desire, but to her own. Until suddenly she was kissing him back as keenly and as wildly. Until just as suddenly she panicked and pushed him away, hard.

He dropped her and she gasped.

'What do we do about *that?*' he demanded.

Kelsi quickly took three paces away, her emotions tossed about like corks on a stormy sea. What was he *thinking* kissing her like that? 'You think complicating this even more is a good idea?' she demanded shakily.

'It's that complicated already. I don't think this is going to make much difference.'

'You've got to be kidding.'

'I still *want* you.'

Absolute fury overruled her. '*You* want *anything* that *moves.*'

His head jerked back, rigid with shock. Oh, she'd overstepped it now. But she didn't care. She could hardly speak for the anger. So angry with him but even more angry with herself—that in this moment, when her life was about to go through the shredder, she was still turned on by him. She was breathless from one itty-bitty kiss, she was thinking about sex instead of the far more serious issue she had ahead of her. That anger made her even bitchier. 'How often have you done it? You take many women there? Is it your usual modus operandi? Take them to the beach and seduce them stupid in the sand?'

'If that was the case, don't you think I'd have had

the sense to carry more than one condom on me?' he shouted back. 'Yes, I've had lovers, Kelsi, but I've never taken anyone else to that beach. I've never done that in the middle of the day like that before. I've never blown off meetings that I should have been in all afternoon just to spend a few more moments with some weird-looking woman who just tried to run me over. It was a first for me, too. These are all firsts.'

Weird-looking. Of course.

'Why don't you just walk away, Jack?' she pleaded desperately. 'I release you from any obligation. Walk away, forget about me. The baby and I will be fine.'

'I can't do that, Kelsi,' he said furiously. 'As much as I would like to take you up on that offer, I just can't do it.'

As much as he wanted to.

Now she hurt even more. 'Why not? You need your freedom, Jack. You like going from season to season. You said yourself your lifestyle doesn't fit with family. And that's OK. This isn't about you. This is about what's best for the baby. Walking away now is the best thing you could do.'

He had to see that this wasn't going to work. That it wouldn't be fair on any of them if they tried to force something that hadn't been meant to be.

He froze, then took the three paces to tower over her again. 'Walking away might be the best option for *you* Kelsi, but it is not for our child. And you will never get me to believe it is. A child deserves to have two parents who love it.'

What—as her father had 'loved' her? Who'd let her down time after time? Her father, a player just like Jack, who'd always put fun before family. And who'd then found a more perfect daughter to replace her.

'Are you capable of loving it, Jack?' she flung back at

him, ancient hurts making her shrill. 'Are you capable of being there for it? Of being responsible?'

When the silence became too uncomfortable she finally looked up at him. He was pale, the energy barely contained in his rigid stance. Kelsi knew his anger before was nothing on the blazing fury he was feeling now.

'I don't need you to lecture me on what kind of parent I should be,' he said, scarily quiet. 'You know *nothing* about me, Kelsi, but I can promise you that's about to change.' He turned. 'I'm leaving now before either of us says something else regrettable. I'll be in touch tomorrow.'

The heavy wooden door slammed, shaking the foundations of the building that had stood rock solid for the best part of a century.

CHAPTER SIX

SHE knew nothing? She knew enough. And Kelsi knew she was right. She didn't want to trap Jack. He had his life, his plans and they didn't fit with family. And she didn't want her child to have a father who wandered in and out of its life—who let the kid down time and time again. She knew how much that sucked. So many times as a girl she'd hoped that her dad would show up when he'd said he would. But he never had. She knew how bad it had felt when he'd found another family he'd rather be with. Rejection like that dug in so deep it was a part of you. A part that was impossible to shed.

Kelsi would do whatever it took to prevent that from happening to her baby. Her baby would be better off without a father at all than one who hurt it like that. And while Jack's intentions might be good, it was only a matter of time before he let them down. So she had to convince him it was fine for him to go—somehow.

But he rang first thing.

'How can I help?' she asked, as if she were a receptionist taking a customer service call.

'Kelsi, don't act dumb. We have to talk.' How could he sound so good-humoured again?

'Actually we don't, Jack.' She braced herself and made

her move. 'In fact I think it's better if we don't see each other again.'

'You what?'

'We should end it all here and now.' She held her breath, waiting for the bomb to explode.

All he did was laugh. 'You actually think that's possible?'

'Sure.' She was so glad he couldn't see her shaking.

'You're not doing this on your own, Kelsi.'

'Watch me,' she said. 'My mother managed. Millions of women manage.'

'You don't have to just manage.'

She gripped the phone harder. Oh, yes, she did. And she would.

The silence curdled.

'I'll be seeking joint custody,' he said, all good humour gone.

Kelsi gaped. The temperature plummeted fifteen degrees with just those few words. 'You're kidding.' He had to be. It would totally ruin his social life. Not to mention all his overseas adventures. This was just him not used to losing, right?

'Not at all. I'm going to be involved, Kelsi.'

She shivered. The temperature was free-falling now—global warming was a myth, the ice age was back.

'Well, OK.' She inhaled. 'You can try to do that.' And if he actually did try, she'd fight him every inch of the way. But she rallied—sure that in nine months' time he'd have lost interest—he'd be consumed by another competition, and another ten or so women to seduce into his bed. 'But until this baby is born we don't need to see each other again. You can contact me through your lawyer after the baby arrives.'

The silence was so long she wondered if he'd hung up. She looked at the phone.

'Kelsi?' He spoke with that sub-zero, too-controlled tone.

'What?' Her nerves snapped one by one, like the strands of a rope being rubbed over a sharp knife.

'Don't think about running away.'

She hung up on him and made herself get ready for work. She went with black contacts—reflecting her funereal mood. Leaving was not an option for her. She didn't want to give up the life she was building here—the reputation for superb performance at work. More than that, she didn't want to go home and confess all to her mother—she'd been so proud of Kelsi's achievements. And Kelsi had done everything her mother had wanted—she'd got out of the small home town, gone to university, gone on to get a great job and rented the tiny-but-cute flat in a fantastic part of the city. She'd done everything the snobs her mother cleaned for had thought she'd never do. And her mother had been pleased and proud of her.

But Kelsi didn't want to face the disappointment now she'd done the one thing her mother had warned her about most strongly. Kelsi knew it wasn't that her mother regretted having her, but that she wanted her to have the freedom and opportunities she'd lost because she'd had an unplanned baby. Kelsi was supposed to do everything she hadn't, not make the same mistake.

She figured Jack's threat was just talk—it didn't really scare her. What really scared her were the feelings *she* had for him. Too long in his presence and she lost her ability to say no. It was those mesmerising blue eyes, the charming smile, the made-for-pleasure body. His magnetism overwhelmed her, causing an undeniable, intrinsic reaction. From the marrow of her bones to the softness of her skin, desire rode in every cell—pushing her to get closer to him. But he lived on the edge, to the max, embracing the thrill…and he liked a lot of thrills.

That was why she didn't want to see him again. She didn't want to be hurt by him the way her dad hurt her mother—with infidelities and broken promises. She *knew* Jack was a playboy—which was fine for a one-night stand, or even a short fling. But he was not for having a family with.

But her own stupid lust confused her and could only make the situation even more complicated. So she had to avoid him. Maybe in a few months she'd be able to handle seeing him again. Surely when she was the size of a house and horribly uncomfortable she'd be totally over wanting him.

Jack's day took a while to improve after his wretched call first thing to Kelsi. He'd hoped she'd have calmed down overnight. He'd tried to, but it had taken him hours to cool off after those last bitter words, but within two seconds of punching her number he was back to viciously angry and threatening things he didn't even know if he meant. *Joint custody?* Where the hell had that come from? How did he think it could even work when he was out of the country for half the year? But all he knew was that he wasn't going to be shut out. She needed his help, whether she liked it or not, and he'd insist she accept it—somehow.

He made himself breathe through the red-rage moment. Because he knew what was driving her anger, what it was that was turning her into such a damn stubborn fool.

She was scared. He didn't blame her. Because so was he.

This was absolutely the wrong thing to have happened. The timing couldn't be worse. He had to focus on getting optimum fitness back if he wanted to compete in the next lot of Southern Hemisphere comps—and he wanted to compete. Like most sports, snowboarding was a younger man's game. If he was going to really pull out something new to take Olympic gold, it had to be now. Hell, he should be in Whistler working on the moves already. So he had to sort this out with Kelsi now.

Kelsi didn't trust him. He didn't blame her for that either. But while she barely knew him, she thought she knew enough to judge him—and that he did have a problem with. Because her judgement was all bad. She'd probably looked him up on Google—didn't she know not to believe everything that was put up there? The injustice of it burned deep. He meant it when he said he'd support her. He already had a good idea about how to begin.

As for that lust? Yeah, it was still there. The rock solid hard-on he got every time he so much as thought of her pretty much proved it. But she thought he was some slut—that he had no standards and would sleep with anyone who offered. OK, so he had some fun but he wasn't completely indiscriminate. More to the point, he *liked* his lovers—he valued friendship. He didn't use people like that—he liked to give as much as take. Sure he didn't—*couldn't*—offer commitment, but he did do respect. And it wasn't as if she hadn't had a good time with him—he very clearly remembered her screaming for him.

Truth now was he hadn't had any for weeks. Four weeks to be exact—since that hot day in the sun. The irony of it all was that she had no idea how badly she'd screwed up his ability to have fun. She wasn't going to know either. He wasn't about to tell her how deeply she affected him—not while she had such a sucksville opinion of him. He'd get over this bone-aching want for her all on his own. But while he cursed the weakness that had brought him back to her, he was grateful for it, too. Now he was here to make sure she would be OK.

He was just going to have to forget the want. Thing was, he was sure she still wanted him, too. For a few, too-short moments, she'd answered the kiss that he never should have taken.

Yeah, it was too bad for both of them.

She was right about not complicating their situation even more but, added to that, her physical well-being was paramount—as much as he wanted her, he didn't want to do anything that might hurt her or the baby. And while he knew sex was OK in pregnancy, he wasn't going to risk it. No complications—physical or emotional.

But he did want her to get to know him better and realise she'd misjudged him. He wasn't going to let her get away with thinking she was the only one who could sort this situation out. He had more to contribute than a couple of chromosomes.

Jack *never* walked away from a challenge—and her trying to deny him had made this so much more of a challenge. And he was damn well going to keep his humour, too—he was all for keeping it fun. That was the whole point of life, wasn't it?

He talked to his lawyer for a while—applying the wax to speed up the ride. It was amazing how money could lubricate deals. They got into the building before lunchtime. The other three apartments were untenanted. As soon as he saw that he knew he needed to move immediately. Kelsi was vulnerable. He wasn't having her stay alone in this big barn in the middle of the city for another night. It wasn't safe.

She wasn't like the other women he'd known: the ones who could throw 920s in the air and laugh about crashing out—strong, survivor types. Kelsi was petite and fragile. And she was carrying his child.

Shudders thudded down his spine every time he thought of that. He—a man for whom a dare was a delight. For whom nothing was worth doing if there wasn't some risk involved. For whom the extreme was the pleasure. He was terrified of her being hurt by something supposedly more natural than any of the tricks he pulled. But then he had good reason to worry, and it was reason in itself to keep his mouth shut. She didn't need anything to freak her out more. Not yet. So long as she saw the best doctor. Team of doctors. Bells, whistles, everything. He'd ensure she was OK, the baby was OK and that they had everything they needed to stay that way.

His lawyer tried to advise an overnight cool-down period, but his mind was made up. He wanted the paperwork signed and the process under way today. The sooner the place was fixed up, the sooner he could feel halfway to free again.

Kelsi took the morning off to see her GP but went to work in the afternoon, sporting the rose-coloured contacts again. Anything to keep some positive in her perspective. Thank heavens for her overflowing inbox. Keeping busy was the only way to cope. She'd manage. She could totally manage all this—somehow—and keeping her job was a key element in her managing.

But when she got back to her home late in the day she saw a big new red Sold sticker slapped across the For Sale sign outside the building. The one she'd been ignoring for weeks now—hoping the building would be on the market for ages yet. Now she was going to have to move? Great.

She checked her box to see if there was a letter from the rental agency. There wasn't. She got to the big door and saw it was ajar. Her pulse accelerated when she heard voices coming from inside. She pushed the door wider and walked to the stairs. There were four men at the top talking. One broke from the group and came down towards where she'd frozen, third step up.

'What are you doing here?' Her pulse just broke the sound barrier with its speed.

'I live here now,' Jack answered, as if it were nothing.

'What?' She managed to look past him and saw one of the men busy staring at the walls and writing things on a notebook.

'I've bought the building.'

'You've *what?*'

'It was for sale. I bought it.'

'Just like that?'

'Cash buyer.' He suddenly grinned. 'Can move things fast.'

She swallowed, trying not to stare, because now his eyes were twinkling and hers were starved for the sight of him. 'What are you going to do with four flats?'

'I'm reconverting it into the one house.'

She gripped the banister to stop herself tumbling back down. 'So you're evicting me.'

He laughed and moved a couple more steps down towards her. 'No.'

Oh, now he'd got close. Too close.

'I'm converting the other three apartments and keeping yours. When the baby arrives you can move into the big space and when I'm here I'll go into the flat. That way I'll be near you both. You can work from home, and I'll be involved with the baby. It's the perfect solution.'

It sounded far from perfect to her. They were going to be under the same roof? He was going to *move in* and be some kind of flatmate? How was she supposed to get over the raunch feelings then?

'Your rent payments cease immediately.'

Kelsi put both hands on the banister.

'It's going to be noisy round here for a while, but I want the conversion done as soon as possible.' He took another step down so he was only one away from her. 'The house will be vulnerable with the renovations going on. Can I move you to a hotel for the next few weeks?'

'No. I'm staying here,' she said firmly. So much was changing in her life. So much was out of her control. And she didn't want him to suddenly be calling *all* the shots like this. This was crazy.

'Yeah, I thought you'd say that.' His lazy smile appeared again. 'I've moved into the one next door.'

'You've *what*?'

'I'm in the flat next to yours.'

He was going to be through the wall? Now? No way.

'You don't need to stay here.' She clamped down on the wayward lick of pleasure curling through her lower belly.

He lanced her with the brilliant sky-blue stare. 'Yes, I do.'

'Not because of me.' She made herself look past him again, but it was pointless—she could feel the magnetism anyway.

'No, I'm sick of hotels. Don't worry.' He bent; his words came as a whisper tipped with a suggestion of sin. 'You won't even notice I'm here.'

As if that were possible. He was six feet of raw, rippled man. And, oh, yes, there was that bit of her that liked the idea of him being so close. Masochistic. That was what she was. She pushed past him and raced up the stairs, unlocking her own little flat and locking it behind her again. She sank onto her sofa, her head in her hands—trying to stop the pounding.

This was all just happening too fast. In less than twenty-four hours her life had been tipped upside down—as if it were a brown paper bag and Jack was the one shaking it to be sure everything had tumbled out and landed all jumbled.

The voices out in the stairwell lingered for a while; she tried to listen, tried not to listen. Then she heard the big door shut and silence returned.

Finally, she could relax. She stretched out on the soft cushions, hoping the churning chaos in her head would slow down enough for her to have a snooze. She was shattered and couldn't be bothered finding anything to eat, too wobbly to talk to anyone—certainly not her mum—and too tired to even cry. She closed her eyes and tried to let it all go, willing the blackness to come swallow her.

The knock on her door chased it away as adrenaline surged. It could be only one person. Only one other person now had a key to get into the building.

She opened the door a fraction, hiding her body behind the heavy wood. He had a way-too-sheepish smile on.

'The oven in my flat isn't working and the power isn't on in the flats downstairs. Do you mind if I use yours?'

'You want to use my oven?'

'I missed lunch.' He lifted the grocery bag in his hand. 'I'm keen for an early dinner.'

'You're going to cook?'

'Yeah.'

She was too tired to argue, just opened the door wide and shuffled back to flop on the sofa. He shut the door and gave her a keen look. She closed her eyes.

'You haven't had any coffee, have you?' he said.

None all day. She had the headache to prove it. She

didn't think caffeine was all that good for the baby. But the first-day withdrawal? It was as if she'd just come down with narcolepsy. 'I just need a rest for a minute.'

He could do what he liked in the kitchen. For a while she listened to the sounds as he did. For a while she tried not to fixate. Impossible. And the dreams were nice—why block them? Why shouldn't she let her mind think on that beautiful body and that beautiful smile, just for a few minutes?

'Kelsi.'

She opened her eyes—stared straight into Jack's. His bronzed, charming face hovered inches from hers—just like in her dreams.

'I have enough to share if you're interested,' he said, all warm, easy encouragement.

If she was interested? Oh, she was so interested—what was he offering, exactly? She gazed at him—the slightly unruly hair that hung over his forehead, the angular jaw that had faint, late afternoon stubble, the creases at the corners of his eyes as he smiled. But then the smile faded.

'Kelsi.' Firmer that time, almost brusque.

She blinked. Slowly the fog in her mind cleared and the rest of her senses switched on. Her mouth watered. 'Something smells good.' She inhaled deep and sat up. 'Something smells really good.'

'Come and see.'

She shook the swimming sensation from her head and followed him to the dining table where the cutlery was set and two plates already in position.

She stared at their contents.

A beautifully cooked prime cut of steak. New potatoes on the side, and in the centre of the table, a bowl of fresh salad with all those extra yummy bits like toasted pine nuts and sliced avocado.

'It's nothing fancy,' he said, sitting down.

It was a lot more fancy than the packet of instant pasta she usually went for. 'You didn't have to do this.'

'I don't like to starve and making enough for you is the least I can do given I just made a mess of your kitchen.'

She glanced through the doorway and he laughed.

'Already tidied it. Figured you wouldn't let me back if I didn't.'

She sat down next to him, tried to steer herself back in the right direction—the independent one. 'But you'll get the oven in your own flat fixed, right?'

'Mmm.' His forking some food in muffled his answer.

She didn't bother with talking either after she took her first bite. This was too good to leave to waste. She'd had no idea she was so hungry. She'd had no idea Jack could cook like this.

'Lots of good stuff here.' He finally broke the silence, nodding towards their three-quarter-empty plates. 'But you should see a doctor. You need to be taking some vitamins. Folic acid and stuff.'

'I didn't know you were a walking baby and birth encyclopaedia.' She took a sip of the glass of orange juice, trying to cool her rising temper.

'I did some research. This is the only child I'll ever have, I thought I'd better get clued up.'

'*I'm* the one having this child, Jack.'

'But we've already established that I'll be there for it.' He grinned, refusing to let her have the last word. 'Starting now.'

She gripped her knife a bit tighter. 'Well, you don't need to worry. I went to the doctor this morning. I have the vitamins and all the information I need.'

'Who's the doctor? A specialist, right?'

Kelsi looked at him, surprised by the insistence in his

tone. 'Just my normal doctor. I'll arrange a midwife in a few weeks.'

'And a specialist. You should have a specialist.'

A midwife wasn't a specialist? What did he want—a whole team of ob-gyns and technicians? Kelsi swallowed hard on the last bit of steak that had decided to wedge in the back of her throat. She wasn't going to start a fight—not tonight. Not until she had the sleep she so desperately needed. 'I'll make arrangements.'

'You don't think you need to ease back on your workload?'

'No.' The urge to argue was harder to suppress now. 'I'm pregnant, Jack. Not sick.'

He sliced his steak with vicious jabs of his knife.

'You don't have to do this with the house.' OK, she couldn't not pick a fight now.

'Yes, I do. You need a home and you like it here. But it's not like you could have bought it yourself.'

No, but in a few years she could have bought a little place somewhere.

'You're never going to have to worry about money, Kelsi, please understand that.'

She put her cutlery down—suddenly feeling as if her stomach was over-full.

'You can trust me.' He practically ground the words out. 'You know what? I trust you. I trust you to take care of yourself and our baby.'

'I have no choice but to do that.'

'I know. And I have no choice but to try to help you as best I can. I will ensure you and the baby are secure.'

But she didn't want to be reliant on him. She didn't want to become too dependant on him only for that support to be whipped away—and it would be. It always was.

'I'm sorry if accepting my help dents your pride.' He didn't sound sorry at all.

Besides, it wasn't her pride getting the battering. It was that thing thumping in her chest. She had to protect it better and knowing more about him might help—like more about his incompatible lifestyle. 'How come you don't have your own apartment to live in?'

Jack stabbed the last bit of his steak. 'I'm never in one place for that long.'

He didn't taste the meat as he forked it in. He just wanted to eat and get out of there. Doing the domestic thing wasn't helping him any. Being this near to her strung his nerves tighter across the wires of want—and he was so close to giving in to it. But he'd known she wouldn't be up to cooking anything—she looked even paler than usual. Tired. Beautiful.

Pregnant.

His guts twisted as he made himself keep that little fact up-front and centre. But it had been so hard not to wake her with a kiss, even harder not to kiss her when she'd blinked, all soft and sleepy—and he'd thought he'd seen heat behind those pink lenses. So he was mad with her, with himself, with this mess.

He'd thought sorting out the house might help. But so far it wasn't because the proximity to her made those weeks of fevered dreams in Canada seem like a saunter on warm sand in summer. To be with her now and not *with* her was nothing but torture. 'I stay in hotels wherever I am.' Hell, he should be in one now. In an ice-cold shower.

'What about the lodge?'

'Karearea?'

She nodded.

So she had done some research on him. What did she think she knew? 'That's a hotel, too.' He shrugged. 'I don't tend to stay there much and when I do I'm just in a guest room.'

'But it's your home, right?'

He shifted on his chair. He didn't think of it like that. Home wasn't a concept he really got. The most comfortable he felt was when he was on the move—on a snowboard, a skateboard, whatever. 'I have a manager to run it. A manager to run the ski field. I'm there a lot in the season. But it's…you know it's just a business.'

He'd been moving from the moment he'd been born, travelling with his dad while he organized all those expeditions for everyone else. The thought of stopping any one place for too long gave him hives. He needed freedom. But he also needed fulfillment. That was some of the drive in his sport—physical achievement filled the sense of emptiness that sometimes swept over him. It gave him focus. But it was another kind of physical satisfaction he wanted now.

'The lodge was my father's plan,' he explained, trying to keep his thoughts in check and not shove the plates to the floor and tumble her onto the table. 'He died before it was finished. So I finished it and got someone to run it. It was an old club field and the club couldn't afford the upkeep any more. It was too remote and they didn't have the resources to put in something that could make it pay. But the mountain is beautiful. The old lift gets you to the top and there's no easy way down.' He managed to grin as he thought of the challenge of those slopes. 'Just a lot of killer options. All advanced or expert level.'

'It's your playground.'

'Sure.' And it was. How he wished he could be there now—fully fit and able to burn some of this frustration off. Anything to tire him out and stop him wanting her so much. 'We have some jumps and boxes and stuff. We put in a half pipe each season.'

'And now it pays.'

'With the lodge it does,' he agreed. 'We're not competing with the big commercial ski fields. We don't want thousands on the snow every day. The pleasure is being the first to shred it after a storm. That's what our clients are paying for.'

The exclusive, high-end of the market who could helicopter in and out and afford the exorbitant rates of the super-luxe lodge. He liked limiting the numbers of people up there—it was too beautiful to be overrun. 'A lot of the internationals like to come and train there because it's private,' he added. 'It's not all about who can afford it. It's about having a place where you've got the space and opportunity to push the limits.'

The international athletes like him. Kelsi nodded, trying to get her head around his oh-so-exclusive world. So he dropped in during the season and then followed the best snow to the other side of the world when summer came here? What a life—chasing your passion like that. Jealousy prickled. So few people had that kind of freedom. She certainly didn't.

But she had a great life, right? She liked the security of having her things around her—beautiful, interesting things and a calm, happy, peaceful life...

But that little twist was already there—worming its way in deeper. Had she missed out on excitement? She'd done nothing but study hard and aim for a good job. Playing it safe all the way. Delaying any plans for travel until she'd established her career. As her mother had encouraged.

It was the right thing to do—and Kelsi had always wanted to do the right thing for her mother. She couldn't compete for her father's attention with her looks, but her academic success had secured her mother's. Kelsi had never wanted to risk losing that approval by sliding off the rails. So she'd never taken a risk at all.

Only now she'd gone off track completely—by accident. And it was too late for any of Jack's globetrotting kind of adventure. In a few months, life was going to be nothing but nappies.

She turned to see Jack putting the dishes into the mini-dishwasher. Wiping down the bench and scooping up a bag of rubbish to get rid of—the picture of masculine domesticity. Except he was doing it with a kind of vicious efficiency—as if he couldn't wait to get out of there. Her limbs ached as she watched him—tall, lean, horribly hand-some. Out of her league handsome. If she hadn't run him over, their paths would never have crossed. Now he'd made sure she'd eaten, he didn't want to stay any longer. It was all uneasy concern—making sure she was OK because he felt obligated.

He was just making the friend effort—thinking it was going to make this mess easier. But he wasn't going to try for anything more between them either. No looks, no touches, no kisses. She was stupid to be so disappointed. It wasn't as if it were a surprise. She wasn't anything like those women who hung out on the slopes. She wasn't beau-tiful or bubbly or super athletic as they were—she didn't tick even one of those boxes, let alone all three.

Men in general didn't find her pretty, so a sex god like him most definitely wouldn't. The afternoon they'd shared had just been a time-filler for him. And that kiss last night? Tactics. Pure and simple. He hadn't liked her trying to shut him out. Thank goodness she'd pushed him away and saved herself the humiliation of having him know how desperate she was for him.

'Thanks for letting me use the kitchen,' he said roughly.

She nodded and stared hard at her orange juice. She didn't want to look at him any more—not with those long legs or the tee that skimmed those abs or the relaxed attitude that tormented her. And with the adventurous streak that all of a sudden she was jealous of.

'Get some sleep.' He all but sprinted to the door.

Her hand tightened on the glass. Great. Nothing but paternal concern—when she was so wired with want she was about to burst.

CHAPTER SEVEN

A WHOLE ton of people arrived way too early in the morning making chainsaw-next-door noise—literally. Less than thrilled, Kelsi staggered out of bed. Despite her early evening exhaustion she'd only fallen asleep just as the bird's dawn chorus had begun. She put in blood-red contacts—to reflect her murderous mood—and stomped down the stairs, slamming the door after her. She'd get to work and lose herself in the creation of something very, very cool and esoteric and new and totally not sport billy.

When she got home from work she saw the old wooden fence had been pulled down and six-foot construction-site fencing was up in its place. Hanging on the temporary entrance gate was a huge chain with an even more massive padlock. Jack was now talking with a man from a permanent fencing company, and a security systems man who had toolbelt on and screwdriver in hand.

She glanced at the house. Yeah, there was a little box with a flashing light near the front door. An alarm system had just been installed. Unbelievable. Had she really thought Jack was laid-back? He seemed to have developed overprotective tendencies overnight.

He strolled over to where she stood glaring at all the upheaval. He still walked as if he hadn't a care in the world, his lithe muscles giving him a look of ease—but she just knew he could leap faster than a tiger, despite the knee. She was not going to let her bones keep wishing he would.

'Am I going to need to memorise some twenty-digit pin number and provide a blood sample just to get in the gate?' She jerked a thumb towards the towering fence.

'Retina scan actually. You're going to have to ditch the contacts.'

She turned her glare on him as he laughed.

'Oh, no!' He mock-horror screeched. 'Couldn't let anyone see what goes on in your head, could you?'

Kelsi pressed her lips firmly together. She was not going to see the funny side.

He walked up the path with her. 'You want to know what I've got planned so far?'

'Not particularly.'

Jack's muscles twitched, keen to haul her close and call her on it. No, Kelsi wasn't going to show a shred of interest in the whole process. He'd never met a woman who wasn't curious about anything and everything. And he'd thought of a way to tease it out of her. One that tickled him.

'I wanted you to meet Alice,' he said as he let her go through the front door ahead of him. 'She's over to talk through some ideas. She's an interior designer.'

Kelsi's features sharpened and Jack swallowed back the smile. Yes, darling, a designer—challenging Kelsi's role head-on. If she was that into personalising her space, then it was time for her to get interested in the rebuilding project—and take hold of the damn olive branch.

Alice walked from where she'd been frowning through the open doorway of one of the downstairs flats. She was one of those glossy-magazine-type designers: all minimal-ist, neutral colours and nothing but the best in fittings and coverings—awfully nice. A bit boring, if Jack was honest, but in person at least she exemplified the absolute opposite of Kelsi's crazy, maximalist, frankly weird, style. She'd hate this yes-woman. Yeah, he watched as they nodded coolly at each other, doing that quick sum-up-in-a-second look that only women could do. Jack had the irresistible urge to tease them both.

'I was thinking about having a fireman's pole put in so we can get from the top floor to the bottom super quick. I thought it would be a good temporary fix while the stairs are rebuilt but maybe we might keep it,' Jack said, gesturing vaguely up to the top floor. 'You know we're gutting the interior completely so this would be useful, don't you think?'

Both women turned to stare at him, mouths ajar.

Alice shut hers and opened it again, as if she were going to speak—but nothing came out.

'Fireman's pole?' Kelsi's voice was a little high, but her scarlet-tinted eyes sliced through him—and suddenly narrowed. 'Great, you'll be able to invite some of your dancing girls over.'

Nice hit. 'Yeah, and I was thinking of red in the library,' he said, loving the bloody look.

'There's going to be a library?' Kelsi sounded amazed.

'Why not? You seem to like books.' He did, too. He might not keep them once he'd read them, but that didn't mean he didn't enjoy or remember them. Whereas it seemed important to her to keep all her things near.

Her eyes widened but she shut her mouth. He heard her teeth snap together.

'A library would be fantastic,' Alice gushed, showing both her clear preference for that over the fireman's pole, and her eagerness to agree on something with him. 'Very now.'

Jack grinned as Kelsi stiffened—Kelsi who was so

damn determined not to agree on anything with him. 'I thought so, too.'

'Will you excuse me, please?' Kelsi mumbled. 'Nice to meet you, Alice.'

Jack excused himself, too, leaving Alice to continue on her mission of absorbing the 'bones' of the house. He followed Kelsi up the stairs, trying not to trip on the eighteenth-century-length skirt she had on—complete with underskirt and overskirt. The assortment of clothes she wore to cover up her body was amazing. At least five layers, maybe eight if he counted the long, lace, fingerless glove things—and he dreamed about peeling every item, oh, so slowly from her. 'I think she'll have some great ideas.' He tried to steer his mind back on course.

'Oh, I'm sure she will.' She viciously flicked through the stuff in the flimsy handbag that hung off her wrist, clearly trying to find her keys.

'Maybe you should show her your place.'

Her handbag and teeth snapped simultaneously. 'I don't think so.'

'You're worried your styles might clash?' As if he hadn't planned it that way. 'Maybe you'd better do downstairs yourself.'

Her chin lifted and she held the key as if it was a dagger, turning to stab it into the lock. 'She'll do a great job.'

Damn, she was on to him. Too obvious.

He leaned on the doorjamb and watched as she fought with the stiff ancient lock. Too obviously close but he couldn't resist. Yeah, he still had the weakness—the unbearable ache to touch.

But now he could see her pulse thudding and her cheeks had gone as scarlet as her eyes. And now, despite the fact the door had just clicked open, she hadn't moved through. What was she waiting for?

Him?

Pure masculine satisfaction heated him as the electricity arced. He could feel her awareness—yeah, the spark was not one-sided. He'd known it, but it was nice to see some more evidence. And how he had the urge to take advantage of it and torment her, because he was sick of being the one on the rack, of wanting, hearing, seeing—but not having her. If she felt even a quarter of the raw ache he felt for her, then he was going to rub some salt in it and make her suffer something of the way he was.

She deserved it—after all she was the one with the off-base judgement. And while he was bursting out of his skin to kiss her and strip her and do a zillion other things, he couldn't.

Unless she caved. Unless she wanted. Unless she asked.

He seized on the idea. Oh, yes, he longed to hear her ask. But if she did, he'd have to be gentle. So slow and gentle and careful. In a single moment he saw it all in his head—how he'd hold her, how he'd touch her, how he'd stroke...

His body was so hard and tight he could barely speak for the pain. He burned to do it now.

But no. He clamped down. No complications—physical or emotional—remember? This was bigger than base needs now. This was a mess that needed sorting as soon as possible—he shouldn't even *be* here. He had sponsors depending on him, other athletes relying on him and his own ambitions to realise. And he'd already ignored three calls from his coach, who no doubt was desperate to know what the hell he was doing.

He had to get himself under control.

He curled his fingers into fists, trying to direct the tension away from his groin. 'You know I'm going to have to borrow your kitchen again tonight. They couldn't fix my oven yet,' he said gruffly.

'No?' she over-the-top exclaimed as bad as he'd screeched before. 'You didn't get that done first thing?'

'Not a priority,' he parried. 'That kitchen is only getting ripped out anyway.'

She finally walked through her door, hesitating a half-second to look back at him before shutting it. 'OK, but make enough for me again.'

He walked back downstairs, smiling grimly. At least he'd got an immediate result in tempting one type of appetite. And he'd make sure she stayed healthy—even if it killed him in the process

Kelsi kicked off her shoes and hit the sofa—end-of-day exhausted again and needing to redraw some strength to handle another hour of Jack.

Playing the happy couple building their dream home together was so not happening. Kelsi knew what he was doing—trying to trick her into giving an opinion, trying to tease her interest. But she was determined. She was not falling for his practised charm. Nor was she going to get used to him being around. Because he wasn't going to be there for long and they both knew it. His knee would get better, he'd be off to some event. She'd be left holding the baby—literally.

And there was no getting past the fact that he wouldn't be here at all if she weren't pregnant. Not good for her ego.

She heard him saying goodbye to Alice out in the yard. Kelsi was sure she was lovely and all, but there was no way they'd agree on anything when it came to decorating this old beauty. Alice would want to put in all the mod things when really what the building needed was to have its original features unearthed and highlighted. Kelsi didn't want to witness what little character was left of the old house being neutralised. Still, she was sure she could rely on Alice to put the kybosh on the fireman's pole idea.

She closed her mind on the X-rated images that popped in thanks to the 'pole', trying really hard to get over the lust thing. Jack obviously had. He hadn't made even a hint of a move since the night they found out about the baby. Not touched her, not looked at her once the way he had that day in the sun. He'd been entertaining himself that day—that was fine. But once had obviously been enough for him.

Shame it hadn't for her. Shame she was burning up.

For some reason she'd thought pregnancy killed a woman's sex drive. Showed how little she knew. It only made hers rampant. Every other thought involved Jack naked and on the beach.

He knocked on her door only twenty minutes later—not nearly long enough for her to put the fantasies in the deep freeze. She opened the door and stood back; even so, he was too close and walked past. His gaze skittered over her, seeming to linger on the little skin she'd bared—her neck, her arms, her hands.

But he strode straight to the kitchen and started prepping—with loud, quick knife skills. His fierce concentration on his Master Chef mission was enthralling.

'Are you always like this?' She pulled a light cardigan around her body to hide but couldn't resist sitting on a nearby stool to watch him.

'Like what?' He didn't look up.

'Like, so focused on whatever it is, making up your mind just like that and going for it full steam ahead, no diversions. No taking it easy.'

'Sure. If a job needs doing you get it done, move on.'

Move on. And she was just another job, wasn't she? Fabulous.

'No point in dragging anything out and struggling over decisions for ages. You've just got to go for it, don't you think?' He tossed something into a pan and it sizzled. 'If you can get the work bit done as soon as possible, then you have more time for the fun.'

Clearly cooking was in the work camp—he was obviously trying to get it done a.s.a.p. 'Fun is everything to you, isn't it?'

'Isn't it for everyone? Isn't that how we should arrange our lives? So we can maximise time for the best bits?' He glanced over to her—his gaze so filled with fire it stole her breath. 'Life is for enjoying, isn't it?'

She didn't disagree completely. 'But isn't there more than just "fun" thrills to enjoy?'

His brows lifted.

'I mean, once you've achieved one thrill, you have to reach higher, harder for another to beat it,' she argued. 'So where does it end? When are you satisfied?'

She understood the drive to create—she had it herself in her own work. But what about creating intimacy, like relationships, or like a home—like life itself? Wasn't that an even deeper way of leaving a mark on the world?

He stopped cooking and stared at her. 'I'm never satisfied.' He turned back to the pan and stirred it viciously. 'Not for long.'

She thought back to that day on the beach—how intense it had been. But how soon they'd both ached for more. No, that satisfaction didn't last.

'There's always another challenge,' he said curtly.

Oh, she bet.

He turned and read her expression. 'Judging me again?'

'Admit it, women are a challenge to you.'

He piled steaming vegetables into a bowl. 'Yeah, I like women,' he said boldly. 'But I like getting to know a lover. I don't just sleep with a woman and then sprint off.'

'Don't you?' Anger swamped her. 'Isn't that exactly what you did that day on the beach? You slept with me and then said goodbye as fast as you could.'

'That was different—'

'It's only different because I'm carrying your baby.'

'Hell, Kelsi.' He tossed down the pan and turned to face her. 'Yes, you're having my baby. I want this to work out—'

'OK, but we don't need to be in each other's pockets to do that. You don't need to be here like this.' She couldn't cope with the way she wanted him—and wanted more from him. 'We don't have to be *friends*.'

He seized her upper arms, jerking her to the edge of the stool, his face right in hers—too close. His eyes narrowed, focused for a second too long on her mouth, on her body—making her burn all the more. Ten, twenty, too many long seconds passed as he used his sensual power to make her suffer in a way she hoped he wasn't actually aware of.

But maybe he was, because his gaze was lingering on her lips again. And she couldn't move for fear of breaking the moment, just wanting him to move those few inches closer. To kiss her. To kiss her with the same blazing passion she had for him.

'You're right.' He released her with a sudden vicious flick of his fingers that somehow bruised her more than a hard shove ever could. 'We don't.'

Shaken, she didn't turn to watch as he walked away. Said nothing to answer his sarcastic parting comment.

'Enjoy your dinner, Kelsi.'

CHAPTER EIGHT

THE TRIBES of builders returned unreasonably early and started ripping down the walls in the ground floor. Kelsi didn't see Jack all day but when she got home that night she found he'd set up some kind of makeshift skateboard park in the mess that was the front yard, with wooden boards making up an assortment of ramps. He didn't appear at her front door to cook dinner for her and it took every ounce of will power not to look out of the window when she heard the scrape of the skateboard on the concrete.

They weren't going to be friends. They weren't going to be anything.

That didn't stop her wanting so very much more in the wee small hours—no, in the smallest hours of the night she lay awake, listening for sounds through the wall. In the smallest hours of the night, when her will was at its weakest, she imagined going to him, touching him.

Only now she never could. Now she knew he didn't want her.

Once more, morning came too soon. As she walked out of the house to head to work he was in the yard already, had clearly just come back from a run.

She glanced at the skateboard under his foot and simply had to try to break the ice. 'Does it help with your snowboarding?'

'Actually, no,' he answered with unnerving gentleness. 'It's completely different. Snowboarding, your feet are fixed to the board. I just skate to relax.'

Oh. Lucky him. She'd give anything to relax right now.

He studied her. 'You're walking to work?'

She nodded. 'I thought it would be a good idea to get a little bit fitter.'

As far as Jack was concerned she was fit already. But he nodded for form's sake. Torn inside about how erotically her dress clung, despite the way its length swamped her and made her seem even smaller. On the one hand he wanted to kiss her desperately, on the other hand he wanted to put her in a cocoon and make sure she was going to be all right. 'You're not walking in those heels?'

She rolled her eyes but then lifted her skirt a couple inches and he saw the Converse All Stars on her feet. Amusement surged in him at the sight of the ultimate skateboarder shoes. So incongruous under her silky old-style skirt. So new they positively winked at him.

'Oh, they're cute,' he said, unable to stop walking right up close to her. 'But they need breaking in.' He slid the skateboard with him lazily, challenging her.

She looked down at it and got what he meant. 'I don't like skateboards.'

But that little smile was there again. He liked that smile. He wanted more of it. It made all the anger of the night before disappear. 'Like you don't like the beach?'

Her teeth crushed her lip.

'Dare you, Kelsi,' he whispered.

The hesitation didn't even last that long. 'Just really carefully.'

Naturally.

'Hitch up your skirt or you'll trip on it.' He'd love it

more if she took it off. He knew this was playing with fire, but how could he resist? That was the whole thing about Kelsi: he couldn't resist her at all.

She hitched her skirt giving him a glimpse of her neat ankles and the slim pale shins. Hell, he was that sex-starved he thought an inch of skin was something to celebrate.

He got her to stand on the board, holding it carefully so it wouldn't slide out from under her. Then, when she had her balance, he carefully towed her. Just a little. Slowly. Watching her feet to make sure she was OK. Then he looked up—and saw the laugh in her eyes that made him want to pull her right on home to him. He couldn't hold back his hunger to look over her body or drink in her fine features.

'I must look ridiculous,' she said, her gaze breaking from his.

He shook his head and tugged her along that bit faster so she had to concentrate. 'You look like you're having fun.'

Her grin blossomed—cheeky, devilishly tempting—spurring him to go faster still. It was stupid—going round and round the concrete pad, but he didn't want to ever stop. But then she wanted a go on her own.

She hitched her skirt even higher, an endearingly serious expression on her face now. She pushed along, steadily building her pace, keeping it straight. He watched her, pleased with how quick she'd figured her footing. He stood in the centre of the yard and watched her slowly circle round him. She was good—maybe her height was a benefit, giving her an easy balance. But he didn't expect her to speed up this much—not so soon. Nor did he expect her to change the angle of her board and take on one of the ramps he'd set up.

'Kelsi!' he shouted, spurting forward to catch up with her.

Oh, God, she was airborne. Years of speed and fast reflexes and sheer grit pushed him forward. His hands reached out to grab and catch her, hauling her to safety. Snug right against his chest.

'Watch your knee!' She shrieked as he swirled around with her in his arms, the skateboard careering off course and smashing into the ragged brush at the side of the path.

He didn't give a damn about his knee. The blood roared in his ears.

'No jumps while pregnant,' he said hoarsely, holding her closer, his heart thudding as if he'd come close to death. The visions in his head shaking him up even more. But as he turned a few more steps the horror faded and he looked down at the woman he was clutching so tight to him.

She was laughing, her head thrown back over his arm, her limbs trembling as she giggled. Her whole body reaction reminded him of how absolute her response had been that day on the beach.

His whole body reacted in kind. His whole body was killing him. He froze. Desperate to control it.

Finally she calmed enough to speak. 'I'm doing that again.'

The protective telling off he'd wanted to shout went unsaid as more primitive urges flared. It would take nothing to hold her that bit tighter and bend his head and kiss her. He could sink to the ground with her in his arms and make her body tremble in even greater pleasure.

'Will you show me how to jump?'

Oh, she had no idea how he wanted to make her jump.

'When you have wrist, knee and elbow pads on, plus

a helmet,' he said roughly. And when she was no longer pregnant.

But he wanted her to do it again, too. The devil in him who loved a dare wanted to see her sparkling some more with her skirt flying and her spirit free, delighted that she'd felt the pure and simple joy of it. But she couldn't—and he shouldn't have let her take even that little risk.

Frustration made him more tense.

He felt her stiffen in response and her smile faded as she looked into his face.

'I'd better get to work.' She looked down, the bloom in her cheeks deeper.

Yeah, she had better get back to her computers and her safe, indoor, insular little world. Because mucking around with the usual regime like this wasn't good for his heart.

Kelsi made her weak body take her own weight. Jack turned and quickly moved to pick up the skateboard—but he shoved it onto the deck. No more riding, then.

Damn.

She walked all the way to work but her body was still on an adrenaline high—feeling more full of energy and zing than it ever had. But it wasn't from the skateboarding, it had been those too few moments in his arms. And she was such a fool, because he couldn't get away from her quick enough.

The yearning was appalling—the never ending need to be near him. But during dinner that night the turmoil was there, a scarce centimetre beneath the surface, and the antagonism between them rubbed the veneer of calm to dangerous thinness. Every look contained a challenge, in every word she searched for a double meaning. And the words grew fewer, the looks longer, until the tension between them silently screamed.

She tried to dig deeper into her defensive trench.

Combating the uncoiling desire by imagining what life would be like when she was living in the big part of the house and he was back visiting—bringing his latest lover to the flat with him.

Absolute torture.

The idea hurt so much she knew that this solution of his wasn't something that she could live with long-term.

She couldn't resist watching out of her window later that night when he was doing more exercises and then kicking out on his board. She wished she were out there, too, with him teaching her some more moves.

She'd never have imagined in a million years that she'd like skateboarding, that she'd want to go so fast and just have some fun. That she'd spend half her life now wishing she could bunk work and go to the beach with him, or boarding or just take off somewhere to do something purely for fun. Because Jack knew how to have fun and she wanted in on that adventure.

But he wasn't offering that.

Finally, thankfully, Friday arrived. She was so looking forward to having the weekend away from work and to the builders not banging downstairs. Hopefully Jack would go away somewhere, too, and she could put herself back together properly and make a decent decision about her future.

As she dragged herself downstairs on her way to work she saw he was up already and waiting for her by the front door. She had to go close to get past him—and he wasn't moving. And as she walked through he stepped to the side—blocking her path completely.

His fingers brushed the smudges under her silver-tinted eyes—she was hoping they'd help her see through the clouds to the lining.

'You're not getting enough sleep,' he said.

She turned away, unable to bear his touch. 'Neither are you.' Shamefully husky. But she knew it was true. He looked leaner and right now he was as pale as the snow he loved.

'Are you sure the builders aren't bothering you?' he asked. 'I've told them not to start until you've gone to work and to stop any loud banging after you get home but I want to get this done as soon as possible.'

So he could get away? 'They don't bother me.'

What bothered her was knowing he slept so near. That was what kept her awake. The unutterable loneliness—the kind of loneliness she'd never felt in all her life, even though she'd been living by herself for over a year now. So near and yet so out of reach.

His knee was better. She'd seen him stretching out this morning—pushing his regime—seen his smile as it hadn't troubled him.

That bothered her, too.

'Have you been feeling sick at all?' He looked into her face, his blue eyes focused closely on her features.

She felt herself flushing. 'Absolutely not.' She faked her answer, faked her smile.

'Kelsi, I heard you being sick ten minutes ago.'

Oh, great. There was no privacy. 'Then why ask?'

His smile was a little grim. 'Just seeing whether you're able to be honest with me.'

Now she felt even worse. 'Jack...'

He held up his hand to shut her up. 'We'll get there, Kelsi. These are the early days, OK?'

'But—'

'Look, I know how hard it is for a parent to bring a child up alone. I'm aware of the sacrifices. You know, if we do this together, maybe we don't have to make the same kind of sacrifices.'

But she didn't want to do this together as friends. Her feelings for him were far too complicated for that. And the more she was getting to know him, those feelings were becoming even more complicated. She leaned back against the frame of the door. 'What did your father sacrifice?'

Jack studied the fence for a moment before answering flat and direct. 'His dreams.'

But that was nothing on what his mother had sacrificed. He clenched his muscles to stop himself crushing Kelsi to him and begging her to please, please, please be OK. The good feeling about how well his knee was working had died when he'd heard Kelsi being sick. He was ready to get back into full training. But she was weakening by the day. So he was trapped and confused and honestly, the whole thing terrified him.

'You mean the lodge? He died before it was finished?'

He dragged his mind back to the conversation. 'Not the lodge, no. That was just a business deal for him. An investment.' Something to put the money into that would make more—and still be related to his life's love.

'So, what were his dreams?'

Jack sighed, his emotions still all over the place. He hated knowing how the pregnancy was affecting her physically. Sure, morning sickness was normal—but it didn't feel normal. It made him worry all the more. But even though he didn't want to talk to her about that, he wanted to reach out somehow. 'He was a climber, one of those guys who climbed any peak. But after...' he paused to clear his throat '...after my mother died he shelved all his plans. He had to look after me and make us some money and the only business he knew was the mountains. He began small—organising tours. One of the first adventure operators in the country. And he was good, business grew.

He started taking overseas trips—to China and stuff. His client base grew—the wealthy in particular. He was good at PR—charming.'

'Like you.'

She said it so soft and quick he wasn't sure if she really had. So he went on—but with his blood running a little warmer.

'I went with him on every trip. He managed it all, team leader, you know? Hired guides, organised agents, ran base camp. But he never went up the summits again—never took the risk. Always stayed safe. As far as he was concerned, I'd lost my mother, and he wasn't risking my losing him too early, as well. So he put his own ambitions on hold until he'd got us financially secure and until he thought I was old enough to deal with it, should the worst happen to him.'

It hadn't taken him that long to get financially success-ful—his father had had the gift—the knowledge and the charisma and the drive.

'And his ambition?'

'Everest, of course.' Jack shook his head. 'Not even the hardest any more, but still the big one. Even though millions have been up there already, he still wanted to.'

'And he never did?'

'He was planning it once the lodge was done. But he had a heart attack—out of the blue. And he never got to do all he'd wanted to.'

Waiting all that time, 'til Jack was old enough, had been a waste, because Jack was never going to be old enough not to feel the pain. Forty-eight wouldn't necessarily have been any better than eighteen had been. And at least at eighteen Jack had already been making money on his own, thanks to sponsorship deals and pro camp wins.

'Do you think he was bitter about not climbing it when you were young?'

'He said he wasn't. He said he didn't care about it as much any more.' But Jack hadn't believed him. Jack had figured that was just his dad making out it was all OK. But as a kid when he'd asked why his dad didn't stand on top of the world like all his clients did, he'd said he had more exciting challenges than that to deal with. That was a line, too. So Jack had learnt the lesson—no putting it off. If you wanted to achieve your dreams, you had to put them first.

His passion was the boarding—but it needed ruthless confidence and no real distractions. If he was going to develop a few more final tricks, he needed to do them in the next year or so. Except now he had this to deal with. But at least he was in a better position than his dad—he had the money already to ensure Kelsi and the baby had the security they needed. He could give her the base that was important. It might not be everything, but it wasn't bad. And he could still focus on his dreams, right? This wasn't going to be the distraction that killed it all. Because he was sorting it so they'd be OK.

'You didn't want to climb?' Kelsi was watching him. He wished he could read the expression in her eyes. Except all he could see when he looked at her was his own reflection.

'It's much more fun coming down than going up. Much faster.' He half smiled. 'I spent my childhood hanging round the mountains—getting my schoolwork done as soon as I could so I could pick up my board and go to it for a few hours. The best.'

'You never went to normal school?'

'Not really. I'd attend in the winter term back in New Zealand, had a tutor when we were on tour. But I went pro when I was in my teens.' He'd done his final school exams by correspondence in the end.

Her frown surprised him. 'What is it you want to do?'

And that was where he and his father differed—his father had wanted to conquer mountains. But most of all Jack wanted to conquer himself. 'That first Olympic gold is mine. And I'll win it with something no one else has ever done.'

Kelsi's silver eyes widened and she leaned closer, asking him with a whisper that did nothing to soften the killer effect of her words, 'And for how long will that satisfaction last, Jack?'

CHAPTER NINE

KELSI heard the knock on the door and hauled herself off the sofa, knowing it was Jack coming to cook dinner.

'Oh, wow.' She stared, her heart seizing. 'Um… um…I…'

Yeah, words weren't possible.

He stepped inside. 'Not what you expected, huh?'

She leaned on the door and watched the back view as he walked into her kitchen. Jack was in a suit. Jack was in the most beautifully tailored tux she'd ever seen outside Oscar telecoverage. Jack was looking so out of this world her eyes watered.

'You're going to cook in that?' she croaked.

'Actually I prepared something last night. It's in the fridge. Just needs heating. You have to heat it up really well, and let it cool, OK?'

Yeah, she got the stop-the-salmonella instruction. Did that mean he wasn't dining with her tonight?

Of course he wasn't. He was in a tux. He was going out. Her heart sank into the abyss. Did he have a hot date or something? With one of those uber-rich babe types who liked to stay at his lodge?

'It's a celebrate sports dinner thing tonight. The rugby guys and netball girls get the gongs.' He winked. 'But we go for the free food and the fans who win the tickets to sit at the table.'

OK, not a date. She breathed a fraction. But there'd be all those talented women there. And diehard fangirls.

And she was so pathetically jealous.

He was frowning as he looked around her room. Suddenly he turned to face her. 'You want to come with me?'

Um. That would be a no.

'I wasn't going to go but the team knows I'm back in town and as half of the others are still overseas, I have to rep them.'

'Of course.'

'So you'll come, too? It's at the gallery. Be a big crowd, but it'll be fun.'

'Oh, no. Thanks.' Could the earth open up and swallow her now. Please?

'Why not?'

Because it was such a last-minute idea. He'd known he had this coming—he'd prepared food for her last night because he'd known he was going out. It was only now he was seeing her look so tragic and alone on a Friday night that he thought he'd better issue a sympathy invite.

'I'm feeling really tired,' she said. It was the perfect excuse—face-saving.

But he looked too concerned.

'I'm fine,' she assured him instantly. 'I'll just have an early night and sleep.'

His frown didn't lighten. 'You'll eat something though, right? You want me to get it ready now?'

'I can manage the microwave,' she said, feeling sicker than she had this morning. 'You go. Go.' She opened the door. 'You don't want to be late.'

'I don't really want to go.'

He wasn't walking out fast enough for her coping mechanism.

'It'll be fun.' She pasted on her best smile. 'Really good.'

Still he stood in the middle of her lounge, not moving. 'You're sure you'll be OK?'

She wasn't an invalid. But she held back her mounting upset and made herself beam. 'Yes. Go.'

And thank heavens, he did.

She ran to the bathroom, her mouth filling with bitter spit. Then she spent five minutes brushing her teeth. Then she looked in the mirror.

She couldn't help wondering about the baby—would it inherit her orange hair and skimmed milk complexion? She sure hoped not, she hoped it would have all of Jack's genes and none of hers. Except that wasn't quite possible.

Poor thing.

He was so handsome. Everything that was perfect. And she just wasn't.

She stared at her reflection, bent forward and took the contacts out and then stood and stared even harder. She'd stopped bleaching her hair the minute she'd found out she was pregnant. So her natural orange was starting to show through already, her skin was paler than tissue paper and speckled all over.

She was what every kid in the playground had called her—a freak.

If she had a sparkling personality maybe that would cancel it out. But she wasn't one of those really outgoing sort who could talk to anyone about anything. One-to-one conversation she could do, but a room full of party people?

No.

And while she might be a damn good web designer, that wasn't exactly a talent that scored accolades.

But the father of her baby wasn't just modelicious-looking, he was seriously monied and an international sporting star. He'd have a million beautiful women throwing themselves at him tonight. And why would he refuse them?

Why would he want her instead of them?

Short answer—he wouldn't. He didn't. He never would.

And that was when—for the first time all week—the tears finally fell.

She went back into her little lounge and curled up with a cushion, burying her face in it as she howled. Knowing damn well she was being pathetic. She was resigned to her looks, was content to make herself 'quirky' rather than cute. But sometimes, just sometimes, she wished she'd been born blonde and blue-eyed and pretty.

This was so one of those times. And where was a fairy godmother when you needed her?

Jack felt as if an army of ants was dancing up and down his spinal cord. He fidgeted as he walked towards the venue, his feet slowing as he saw it in the distance. He really didn't want to go there. Not without Kelsi. He'd hoped she might say yes to coming with him. He knew she liked art and the function was being held in the city gallery. But she'd shied away from the invite. Even though he'd deliberately kept it casual, she'd still said no.

Hell, he should have said no, too. He didn't feel like seeing the other guys. He just wanted to be with Kelsi. He was tired of fighting it. They had to get to some better arrangement—he had some feelings that were worsening, not lessening. Denial wasn't doing it. He stopped in the middle of the path and thought for another split second.

And then he turned around. As the house came back into view he imagined it whole again, imagined it filled Kelsi-style—with that warm, welcoming chaos that somehow he'd gotten used to. There was security in all that stuff. She'd make it such a great home. A funny feeling splintered his chest and he realized something—his baby was lucky.

She didn't answer when he knocked. But her door wasn't locked and he couldn't not check on her. Surely she couldn't be asleep already—he'd been gone less than half an hour. He'd just peek and see.

She was on the sofa, tucked into the cushions. Maybe she was asleep. But then he saw her shoulders move.

'Kelsi?'

She jerked up, swiftly turning away from him. 'What are you doing back here?'

'I didn't—' He broke off and saw her shoulders shudder again.

She was crying.

'What's wrong? Is something wrong?' His heart pounded faster than the first time he'd attempted a 1080 and smashed down flat on his face.

'Please go away,' she mumbled.

'No. You're upset.' This was worse than when he'd heard her being sick this morning. This was like watching someone swallowing broken glass and not being able to stop them.

'Jack.' She put her fists to her face, hiding the fast-flowing tears. 'Can't you leave?'

He went and found a flannel, ran it under cold water, and stalked back to the sofa. She hadn't moved. He sat right next to her and forced her hands from her face, holding the flannel to her eyes—trying to be gentle.

Her half-sobs stopped, but she kept her eyes closed.

He turned her towards him with his fingers on her chin. 'Kelsi, please look at me.'

Colour flashed.

He drew in a sharp breath, the surge of need rising so fast, blasting all thought from his head. 'Oh, my God.'

He dropped the flannel, framing her face with his hands as he gazed into her beautiful, bare eyes. So hungry to see them.

Leonine—gold—the most unusual pale gold. 'Why do you hide them?' He was so incredulous his words whispered out instead of roaring as he'd meant. He just couldn't understand why she would. They were so unique. So beautiful. Just like the rest of her.

'Why are you here?' she said angrily, twisting free from his grip. 'You're supposed to be at that dinner.' She sniffed and grabbed the flannel from her lap, hiding her eyes from him again.

He tried to gather his scattered wits. 'Is it because of the baby? Is that why you're so upset?' He desperately wanted to know. He desperately wanted to help. He desperately wanted to gather her close and cradle her and tell her it was all going to be all right.

She shook her head. 'I'm just tired, that's all.'

He didn't believe that was all it was. But he didn't know how to fix it. She was inching away from him. Not even that subtly, moving farther and farther away.

Oh, hell. Did she feel that helplessly trapped?

God, they needed to get out of here. He could really do with some air.

He frowned. Come to think of it, she hadn't been out once all week—aside from work. Sure, he hadn't either but he'd been texting his friends and caught up with a couple during the day. But Kelsi's phone hadn't rung once. He knew she was quiet—that was OK—but lonely wasn't so good.

And she shouldn't be lonely. She should have a ton of friends. She was fun company—bright, with a sharp sense of humour that appeared when you least expected it. Yeah, he got that she was a little shy—the kind of work she did told him that. She hid behind a computer screen and emailed rather than talked face-to-face. But she could get over that...

'You should go to the function,' she said gruffly. 'You can't just not show up.'

'Why not?' He shrugged. 'I wasn't going to be there originally.'

'But they're expecting you now. Those people have paid money or won competitions to be there.'

Yeah, he knew that, didn't need to be made to feel worse about it. Actually it was her wanting rid of him that made him feel worse. 'I'm not leaving you alone when you're like this.'

She looked cross. 'I'm not helpless, Jack. I'm fine.'

'Prove it, then,' he said coolly. 'Come out with me.'

'No.'

'You haven't been out all week,' he said firmly. 'You can't spend your life at home.'

She was sitting very still a clear foot from him.

He leaned across and brushed her crazy hair back from her cheek. 'I'm not going unless you go with me.'

She leapt up from the sofa as if his hand had burned like the sun. 'I can't. I haven't anything appropriate to wear.'

Oh, that was a pathetic excuse. 'What do you mean, not appropriate? All your clothes are appropriate.'

'Not for a black tie event.' She whirled to face him, her golden eyes glittering—killing him. 'I don't have a fairy godmother. There's no one to give me a makeover to go to the ball.'

'You don't need a makeover,' he said automatically, still stunned by her eyes. 'You're perfect as you are.'

But now those eyes filled again. 'Don't say that.'

'It's true.' He stood, needing to get it through to her somehow—like with a battering ram or something. 'I'm not making it up, Kelsi. I'd be proud to have you walk in with me.'

She stared at him as if he was a lunatic. The ants danced down his spine some more. And his instinct told him he needed to get her out of there, that he needed to take her with him. 'Just go and get dressed. Wear any of your dresses—all of them at once if you want,' he joked lightly. 'Just come out and have some fun.'

He breathed in, waiting. But she seemed to be waiting, too.

'Please.' Did the sound come out on that or had he just thought he'd said it? He really wasn't sure because his mouth had all dried up.

But she'd turned. She'd walked.

And he was waiting.

Kelsi went back to the bathroom and breathed in deep. Jack wasn't going without her. That was clear. But she didn't have a ball gown and there'd be all those amazing sportswomen there with their strong, fit bodies and their tanned skin and their glamorous hair and make-up. And she just couldn't believe his 'you're perfect' line. Too smooth.

Too tempting.

And worse still, she couldn't put in any contacts now. Her eyes were sore and red from crying and they'd only water more if she tried to put them in. She was going to have to go out with naked eyes. She hadn't done that in such a long time.

She should feign illness. Plead exhaustion.

Except there was that yearning—reaching up from her most secret self. She really did want to go. To go out with him just the once. To be the one on his arm even for only one night. To be the one he wanted to be with.

And she was too tired to fight the fantasy.

She turned the shower on and jumped in, quickly washing away the stains of the day. She twisted her hair up, hiding the worst of it and skimming some make-up over her face. Then she went in search of a frock.

He was standing at the lounge window when she emerged from her bedroom. And, yeah, it was the fantasist in her that saw his whole face light up.

He held the door open for her. 'What do you call this?' He brushed the feather she'd pinned in to half hide the mess of hair exploding from her high ponytail as she walked past him.

'A fascinator.'

'Very appropriate.'

See—his charm would see him win every time.

He'd called a cab and it was already outside. Nervously, she tucked her dress in close so its skirt wouldn't get caught in the door. It was one of her long ones, of course. But she'd skipped a few layers—including her bra—because it had a peephole in the centre of her back. For once she let it peep all the way to skin, not another layer. And her arms were bare. She basically felt naked.

'You're going to meet some of the guys. I have to warn you they can be a bit extreme,' he said as he joined her in the back seat.

'In what way?' She tried to keep her breathing regular.

'Oh, you know, a bit crazy.'

'You have to be crazy to do what you do.'

'Yeah, the snowboarding table is always at the back of the room.'

'So if you make too much noise it's not so far to throw you out?'

'Not me.' He laughed. 'Them.'

She bit her lip—she wasn't a party queen. And she couldn't even have a drink to help her relax. This was just madness.

The place was full already, of course. Pre-dinner drinks were almost over, which was perfect timing because they could just slip into the crowd rather than make any kind of grand entrance.

'That's them over there.' Jack waved to a guy across the room and took her hand to draw her with him. There were a bunch of them, all in suits but some with personalising features—big hair and beanies seemed to be the order of the day.

Jack got waylaid three quarters of the way across the room by some other big, tall, fit person but she glanced over and saw the snowboarders were watching them, and now walking nearer to meet up with them. She half turned to Jack to listen to him greeting the guy who she now recognised as a rugby star. But the low conversation easily came to her ears as the beanie brigade neared.

'Check out the woman Jack's with.'

'Sick.'

'Yeah.'

Kelsi stiffened. They thought she was sick? OK, so she had pale skin, so what? That didn't mean she was at death's door or anything. She shouldn't have left her arms bare. She shouldn't even be here.

'You OK?' Jack asked quietly, turning to her after a big laugh with the rugby dude.

'Sure.' She made herself smile.

'Come and meet the guys.'

Reluctantly, she stepped up as he introduced her. Tahu, Drew and Max—who all stood smiling and silent and staring at Jack as if he was better than Father Christmas.

'Max is the current boardercross champ,' Jack said with his wicked grin.

'Boardercross?' Kelsi asked

'You get four guys going straight down an obstacle course as fast as possible. First to the bottom wins. Take no prisoners,' Jack explained. 'Tahu and Drew specialise in superpipe.' He looked over at Drew. 'How was Silverton?'

'Sick.' Drew answered Jack direct with an almost shy smile. 'Tori pulled another McTwist and then nailed her first 720.'

'Wow.' Jack's brows lifted. 'She's been after that for ages. Is she here?'

'Should be soon.'

Kelsi tugged on Jack's sleeve. 'You're going to have to translate again for me.'

'McTwist, 720, 1080, all tricks—jumps and turns you make on the half pipe.' Jack twirled his finger in the air.

'And they're "sick"?' Kelsi really needed that one clarified.

'Awesome, fantastic, rad.' Thesaurus Jack offered some synonyms.

So 'sick' was a compliment in snowboard speak?

Kelsi flushed, felt her smile go natural.

Jack put his hand on her back. 'The slang is a little OTT.'

'You don't snowboard?' Drew asked, amazed.

Kelsi shook her head, unable to speak because Jack's hand had slid a little higher up her back and now his thumb was stroking over that small spot of bared skin.

'You have to go,' Tahu said. 'Do it once and you're hooked.'

Rather like riding Jack himself. Oh, she so had to get a grip on herself.

'Jack'll show you,' Tahu added.

'Yeah,' Drew agreed, utterly serious. 'He's the master of big air.'

Jack led her away with a slightly pained expression.

'He meant *hot* air,' Kelsi teased, wriggling away from Jack's marauding thumb.

His arm went right around her waist and he pulled her close. 'Very funny,' he muttered in her ear.

He took her to talk to the fans there to meet him. But as they all came together again to sit down for dinner it struck her that the other snowboarders were just as much fans of Jack's as the people who'd paid to be there. They all watched him, they all hung on his every word. Beside her he rested his elbow on the back of her chair, leaning close as he listened and answered the zillion questions that came from both fans and fellow athletes. Quietly humble and polite in the face of all the adoration.

His attention to her was all politeness, too—he was just being nice, friendly, ensuring she was having a good time. Which she was. He was the perfect PR charmer—who she was so hopelessly attracted to.

Just as the formal part of the evening came to an end, a woman appeared—welcomed with cries from Tahu and Max about how typical it was for her to be so late. She was medium height with long blonde hair, blue eyes and smooth, clear, freckle-free skin. Kelsi gazed at her in awe.

'This is Tori—New Zealand's future slopestyle queen.' Jack introduced the girl who was smiling so brightly at him.

This girl wouldn't just be the queen of snow, she'd be the queen of the world. Just as Jack was the king. It wasn't midnight but the dream was over already—Kelsi was the pumpkin in the presence of the real princess. Tori was everything Kelsi wasn't. And not just in looks—she was sociable, talented and successful in a field others were actually interested in. She had it all.

Kelsi looked around the room and saw all the other fit, fit bodies—male and female. Good genes and talent and determination oozed from all these absolute champions. And the fun she'd felt only moments before tumbled away.

She was so out of place.

'Dance with me.' Jack couldn't wait a second longer to get Kelsi in his arms. To wangle it so he could feel some more of her soft, smooth skin again.

She obliged, but she wasn't focused on him. She was too busy star-spotting and determinedly *not* looking at him.

'There are a lot of really gorgeous women snowboarders, aren't there?' she commented. 'Like Tori. They're all so beautiful and nice and amazingly talented.'

'You're more beautiful,' he said simply.

He watched the colour flow in her cheeks and her lips tighten. She didn't believe him. She was really that insecure? He'd seen the way she'd fidgeted with her dress when she'd seen the short-skirt numbers of the netballers. He thought her outfit was far more flattering in the less-skin-is-more kind of way. Although right now he wanted more skin for sure. But she wasn't comfortable in it, was she—just being in her own skin?

Suddenly he saw what the problem was. The completely obvious obstacle that had made her try to put up all the stop signs the minute he'd walked back into her life.

She didn't think she was hot.

He swore under his breath and had to consciously relax his hold on her. Didn't she realise he was the envy of every guy here tonight? That they all wanted to tuck her into their pocket and carry her off somewhere private to do wicked things with her?

He watched her eyes flicker again as another six-foot netball Amazon strutted past.

Everything crystallised.

She'd accused him of wanting 'anything that moved' because she didn't think she was pretty enough to attract him. She thought that he'd only hit on her that day because she was there—the nearest body to scratch the itch he had at the time.

Good grief.

Insulting to him, yes. But even more insulting to herself.

Fury rose—who hadn't told her how beautiful she was? How incredibly sexy? More than that, how attractive she was *underneath* the skin—how interesting, fun, sweet, talented, *strong*. Yeah, she was unbelievably strong and determined and bright and articulate… He could go on and on and on because she really did bewitch him. And he couldn't believe she didn't believe it.

She was an amazing woman, who should never have lost her confidence in herself like this. He hated whoever it was who hurt her so badly. He wanted to know who and why and how. He wanted to slam out the insecurity.

Desperate desire hurtled through his body, testosterone

snapping every muscle to tight tension. And with it came the single-minded determination he was famous for.

He'd prove it to her. He'd prove her gorgeousness. Tonight. Over and over and over again.

CHAPTER TEN

'WE SHOULD go home, Kelsi.' Jack coughed to clear the rasp from his voice.

'It's still early.' She turned, surprise flashing in her eyes.

He could gaze into those eyes for hours. Why did she cover them up all the time? He was going to find out. He wanted to know everything.

'My knee's feeling it a bit.' Well, not his knee exactly.

'Oh, you should have said sooner.'

The taxi didn't drive fast enough for him. He secured the alarm as quick as he could, then followed her up the stairs. Waited while she unlocked the door to her little flat, standing close enough to see her pulse breakdancing—which didn't help his 'knee'.

But she wouldn't look at him. 'Um, did you want something?'

'Yeah.' He pushed her door open and walked inside. He slid off his jacket and pulled his tie free. The top button of his shirt was already undone. 'I'd really like to kiss you.'

She was standing by the wall, still near the door. Now she pressed her lips together, her eyes avoiding his.

'I haven't slept with anyone since you,' he said bluntly. 'I don't want to sleep with anyone but you.' He really wasn't that pleased about it but it was the absolute truth. 'I want you and only you, OK? And not because you're the nearest breathing woman. I want you because I think you're beautiful.'

She said nothing.

'You don't believe me, do you?'

She still didn't answer. Her hands curled into fists, her whole body locking into a hopeless, defensive pose.

Jack breathed in hard and pleaded with his body to slow down. Jumping on her this very second probably wasn't the best idea—even though it was the one both his brain and body really wanted to fixate on. But Kelsi needed more than that—she needed some serious convincing. That meant words as well as actions. And those actions had to be gentle—remember? He rubbed his hands over his face and summoned some control. And some courage.

'You want to know what I see when I look at you?' Did she want to know what he thought?

She flashed a look at him. Lightning quick before she went back to studying the floor. But she was listening. She was utterly immobile as she listened.

He swallowed. Hoped his voice was going to hold out for him. 'First up, overall impression is this really feminine woman. I see your collarbones—delicate fine bones covered by this smooth skin that slopes to those breasts that jut out just the right amount. Then there's this narrow ribcage that goes to that even narrower waist, and then you have those curving hips.' He paused to take another deep breath. Talking this way was just killing his body—winding him tighter than he'd ever been. But he had to make her understand first, then he could *do*. 'You're petite and perfectly formed. You have these tiny ankles that I can fit my hand around. I remember doing that in the water when I pulled your leg higher round my waist. Your skin is so smooth, so soft…' He badly wanted to touch that softness now. 'And then there's your face. The first thing I saw that day and I thought it was the most stunning face I'd ever seen. These *angles*.' He tried to make her understand. 'You've got these cheekbones, and your wide eyes were filled with tears, and you have the perfect tilt to your nose.' He sighed. 'Then there's your mouth. Big, soft lips that first trembled and then kissed me so sweet. And your crazy curls that defy any attempts at control. I like that about your hair. It's a lot like you as a whole…' He smiled at her, beginning to really enjoy the confession—the acceleration of his heart and the pumping of his blood. '…and you as a whole just makes me think sex. I see your smile, I see the way you lift your chin and I want in.' He began to lose the battle of control over his body, his voice going totally rough. 'And I'm so tired of this Eiffel Tower erection I've been sporting for months.'

'You really haven't…?' She finally spoke. But she couldn't finish her sentence.

'I really haven't,' he said flatly. 'Feels like a hell of a long time.' He walked to where she leant against the wall, her hands twisted together in front of her waist. And he saw the colour suffusing her face. The way she was shyly watching him—almost believing him. He'd damn well make sure she believed him by the end of this night.

'And I see your smile, Kelsi.' His voice did crack then. 'I see the twinkle in your eyes even though you do your best to hide it. I hear your laugh, your teasing words, the fun that bubbles out when I least expect it. The passion and playfulness like you had that day on the beach—I ache for it. Wait for it. Want it.' Oh, how he wanted it.

'So now you know what I see,' he said softly. 'You want to know what I want to *do?*'

Kelsi swallowed. Couldn't move as Jack rested his hand

on the wall beside her head and leaned closer to whisper even more softly.

'Shall I tell you what I'm *going* to do?'

Pleasure rippled, contracting every muscle in her body. She closed her eyes. It was words, just words. And she'd seen tonight just how charming Jack could be. How social. How smooth.

'I play it in my mind all the time. What I'll do first when I finally touch you again.'

Oh. Her eyes prickled and she screwed them tighter shut. She was not going to cry—even though she really felt like it.

'I think a kiss—mouth-on-mouth. I ache to lick along your lips, to feel the softness on the inside. But I don't want it to get out of control too soon so I'll pull back. There's too much else to worship.'

Worship? He wanted to worship her? Her breathing slipped. He was right in front of her now. She could feel his heat. She opened her eyes but couldn't look right up at his face. His other hand was on the wall, too—so she was almost within his hold. His body centimetres from hers—and the tension was radiating from him as powerfully as heat radiated from the sun.

'I want to tangle my fingers in your curls and pull your head back so I can kiss down your neck to your collarbones.'

Instinctively her neck arched just a fraction. She could feel it, she could almost feel the touch—she badly wanted to.

'I'll undress you. Slide the straps from your shoulders. Can't wait to watch the material fall to the ground so I can see you again.'

Her lips parted as she struggled to keep breathing regularly, desperate for oxygen.

'And you know what, Kelsi? I like freckles. I want to join all the dots with my tongue.'

Goose bumps burst as she shivered—would he warm those, too? Her nipples pressed harder against her dress. She wished it were off. She wished she could blink their clothes away and she could be in his arms and believing it all.

'I'll skim my fingers over your skin—lightly, so I can feel the silkiness. But part of me wants to grab at the same time. Clutch you closer to grind hard and quick. Somehow I have to keep it slow.'

His voice was low, rough, *honest.* Obliterating every last little brick of her defence. She closed her eyes again—to listen all the better, to feel it.

'So I'll kiss you all over, too. Suck on the sweet bits you like to keep hidden.'

Those bits tensed, merely the thought teasing them— making the rest of her yearn for the reality.

'But I want inside so bad. Hot, tight honey.'

She was burning up now—her body clenching on just his promise.

'Even more I want to see you, hear you, feel you convulsing under me. Around me.' Almost sounding angry now, he whispered hot and fast, the words tearing free from him. 'I want you to scream and cry and laugh. I want to thrust so deep inside you break apart. I want it to be me who makes you like that. Me who frees you. *Me.* Only me.'

Blood pulsed. Thundering in her lips. In her sex.

His mouth was right beside her ear as he roughly demanded, 'Do you understand now how much I want you?'

'Jack…' She couldn't stop trembling.

'Do you understand I'm going to do it all right now?'

Her eyes shot open as she jerked involuntarily. Looked into his huge, dark eyes, blazing with the desire he'd so devastatingly detailed.

'Please.' Her voice broke, and she pressed her fingers hard into her palms. She needed the release so badly. She needed him so badly.

She longed to believe him. To feel him. To know for sure.

'Jack.'

His gaze burned into her eyes for a second—an age— longer. And then he looked at her mouth. Her thirsty, desperate mouth.

She drank him in—the hint of sweat on him, seeing the way he, too, was struggling to control his every breath. His every move.

It was so slow. So deliberate. The lean that brought his face close to hers once more.

'Kelsi…'

As he breathed her name their mouths finally met. She moaned, her body curled, muscles crunching as a mini-orgasm stunned her.

With a groan he swiftly moved to support her, his hands strong and firm in their hold.

'Oh,' she nearly cried as she fell against him. 'I feel really hot, Jack.'

He licked her lips as he'd promised. 'I know you do.'

She licked, too, twirling her tongue round his. It had been too long. Was too slow now.

His hand swept through her hair, tilting her face so he could kiss every inch—down her jaw, her throat, to her collarbones. He groaned again and involuntarily pushed forward, bumping harder against her. Oh, how she wanted to feel him all the way inside her.

'Slow,' he ground out.

'No.' She kissed him—a long, long kiss where she offered and gave but most of all took. Took everything he offered—everything he had.

He wrenched his mouth from hers, their hot, quick breaths gusted between them in the split second before he shoved her straps down, the dress ripping as he yanked it from her body.

His hands on her breasts made her cry out, her fingers curled into useless claws as the sensations momentarily paralysed her.

He went tense, too. 'You OK?'

'Yes,' she panted.

He bent, moving his mouth over her. Her nipples were hard enough to cut glass and the sensations of his hot, wet tongue sent her insane. She had to get him naked. Her naked. Now.

But her fingers still failed. Trembling, panting, she half pleaded with him. Felt relief as she felt him hook her knickers. As he slid them down he knelt before her.

Kelsi had no choice but to lean back against the wall, her vision tunnelling as she looked down and watched her ultimate lover press his open, adoring mouth to her.

'Jack.'

He glanced up and caught the look on her face.

'Kelsi.' He reached for her waist and took her to the floor.

She curled around him, clinging, unwilling to release him even to let him take off his clothes. She loved the kisses too much. The deep, delicious hungry kisses that made her feel as if he'd been aching to hold her like this for ever. The way he moved so ardently over her. As their mouths clung, his hands moved, undoing, trying to ease fabric aside. But still it wasn't enough. He growled and pulled away so he could strip completely.

She watched, impatient, fascinated, desperate.

At last he rolled back, pulling her beneath him and bracing above her. Taking too long. Taking way too long.

His blue eyes devoured her, brilliant, intense, stunning. Honest—so honest in revealing his desire. In that timeless moment before his body claimed hers she was suspended in a bubble of other-world excitement, of disbelief as she saw he'd meant every passionate word.

'OK?' he asked.

'Oh, yes.'

She burst apart the moment he pushed into her. Her whole body a mass of quivering muscles that clamped on him, that released for the merest of seconds before clamping tighter again. It was like being totally submerged in a sea of heat and light and colours too brilliant to absorb. Eyes screwed shut, she cried out as she clung to him, unsure she was going to live through the intensity.

'It's not finished yet,' he grated harshly, holding her close as she violently shook beneath him. 'I won't let it be. Not yet.'

Kelsi breathed carefully, her shudders easing as the sensations slamming inside her ebbed. And then he thrust deep—controlled, slow, his face rigid with the strain as he worked to bring her out again. But now Kelsi was all smooth and fluid and sure. Utterly replete, she arched up to him, sinuously rocking, not letting him keep the control he seemed so bent on. Refuelled by his flinching response, she forced a faster pace, faster still until his muscles bunched even more. She laughed delightedly as his eyes flashed pure fire and his face puckered under the strain of a pleasure that was almost pain. He breathed in sharply.

'Jack,' she said as she was submerged in the delight again.

Suddenly all the energy inside him poured out in a frantic, furious ride. He pumped so hard all she could do was wind her arms and legs around him and cling tight— swept back into the stormy oblivion that was strong enough to stop her heart altogether.

All power. All grace. All consuming. He was all there was—all she could see, hear, feel.

Her everything.

CHAPTER ELEVEN

IN THE blackness, sound returned. The thumping of her heart, the rush of her breath. Then the light came back, too, as Kelsi lifted her lashes and focused.

Jack was still with her. Only now he took more of his weight on his arms so she wasn't so crushed.

'Beautiful Kelsi.' He kissed her—her lips, her face, her neck, all over. Soft, sweet, reverent passion. 'You're OK?'

She nodded contentedly. And then, despite her thinking she had zero energy left, she kissed him back, running the tip of her tongue along his lips, teasing them open some more so she could explore his mouth. Long, luscious kisses that were slivers of heaven.

He broke apart, moved to kneel beside her. 'In a bed this time. In bed all night.' He gathered her into his arms and carried her to her bedroom.

He was relentless in his attention. In the words he whispered throughout the night. In his pursuit of her pleasure.

She had no hope of holding out—and no desire to. She totally succumbed to the feelings she had for him, submerged in the sensations he pulled from her and the bliss of believing herself to be utterly desired. For the first time in her life she felt beautiful and special and sexy.

As the new day advanced so did her sense of confidence—of fun. She took the time to tease him—to ride astride him as she'd done that wild day on the beach. Mesmerised, she made his muscles bunch and ripple and shake in a way that was so far beyond his control. She glowed as she felt the power and pleasure of being attractive.

Together they lost time in the exploration of each other. It was magic—beyond thought, word or touch. Simply sensation.

'Are you OK? You're sure you're OK?' He asked after he'd done a kitchen raid for both salty and sweet supplies in the early afternoon. 'Not too tired?'

She shook her head. 'Just don't ask me to get out of bed today. Other than for a shower.'

'A shower and then straight back to bed,' he said firmly. 'Bed all day tomorrow, too.'

She giggled, more inclined to move on him than to argue at that moment.

The sun shone in through her window, sending a sheet of warm, bright light diagonally across the bed. She stretched out in the middle of it, for once letting the warm rays soothe her sensitive skin.

He lay on his back, his hand resting low on his abs as his chest rose and fell fast as he caught his breath. But his gaze didn't leave hers. She knew—because hers didn't leave his.

'Why do you hide your eyes? They're the most amazing colour.'

She sighed and then rolled, reaching for her phone on the bedside table. She scrolled through a few pictures and then showed him one. 'This is my mum.'

He studied it. 'Wow, wouldn't have guessed.'

No, her mother had light-brown hair and blue eyes. 'So who do you think I look like then?' she asked.

'Oh.' He looked awkward. 'Your dad. And he's…?'

'A jerk,' Kelsi said. 'Yeah.'

He reached out and touched her shoulder. 'How so?'

'He just… He cheated on Mum and she took him back and he just let her down again. It went on and on until he finally left us for good. I hate looking in the mirror and seeing him look back at me. He brought nothing but disappointment.'

'Are you in touch with him now?'

She flicked through a couple more pics on her phone. 'This is him here.'

She waited while Jack looked at that one.

'Who's he with?'

'His stepdaughter. She's the same age as me.' And pretty in the world's most conventional way. She'd gone on to study law and commerce at university—he was so proud of her.

'Really?' Jack handed the phone back.

'He went to her graduation. He bought her her first car. He gave a speech at her twenty-first…' Kelsi pulled the sheet up to cover herself.

'And he did none of those things for you.'

He'd said he would. But had he? 'No.'

He hadn't shown up to either the twenty-first or the graduation. He'd let her down so many times before that, she shouldn't have been disappointed. But she had been. Always she'd wanted to believe he'd be there for something that really mattered. And he never had.

'He's hurt you a lot, huh?' Jack said softly.

She shrugged to minimise it. 'Parents are supposed to stuff us up, right?'

'Parents are supposed to support their kids. Not be selfish.'

She looked at him—saw him freeze as they both suddenly thought of their own child, slowly growing inside her. They had a huge job ahead of them—and they had conflicting wants for the future. Now they'd complicated it all the more by bringing their lust into the equation.

Doubt surfaced the way a mythical monster rose from a picture-perfect lake—sudden and terrifying. What were they doing sleeping together like this? Where was it leading?

She knew already. Because while he'd made her feel so wonderful with his hot words and praises, there'd been no promises.

Kelsi sat up, moving away from him. And for the first time in fifteen hours, he let her.

She walked into her bathroom, knowing she needed to put the brakes on her infatuation. Just because the man thought she was attractive, she didn't need to think herself in love with him or anything. She needed to watch herself.

But Jack appeared in the doorway, coming to stand behind her as she frowned at herself in the mirror. His hands settled on her body—smoothing.

'You're not your mum, Kelsi, and not your dad. Just you. And your eyes are beautiful. Be proud of them.'

She turned and shushed him with her mouth. She didn't want those words any more—the ones that made her fall all the more for him. Recklessly she fired up her movements. She had to make the most of the moment. Because the moment couldn't possibly last.

Through the night Jack let her take the lead—both physically and in the avoidance of discussing anything too heavy. He didn't want to think of anything more than a few minutes ahead.

She pushed them both to a new frontier of high-speed, high-endurance sex that had her clutching the bedhead for support and him feeling like beating his chest and roaring like a victorious warlord. She stunned him with her strength and stamina and sparkle.

He'd known, hadn't he? He'd known how passionate and beautiful and bewitching she was. How wild. And he was so damn glad he'd worked out how to unlock it all again. He buried himself in her, buried the thoughts of what else he ought to be doing. He just wanted to be with her.

But on Sunday morning, she pushed him away. 'I have to work on a design. I have a deadline this week. I can't waste another day with you.'

Waste a day? Um, no, he damn well wasn't *wasting* a day either. He didn't have time to. So he wasn't going anywhere. But he could make a compromise. 'I could help you.'

'No, you can't,' she said firmly. 'You're a distraction.'

'I won't be. You need to take regular breaks from the computer or you'll get RSI.'

'I need to concentrate.'

'I'll be quiet. In fact I'm going to sleep. I'm tired.' He snapped his eyes shut. 'You go work for a few hours out there.' He felt her hesitation. 'Go on,' he said brusquely. 'Stop wasting time. Get chained to the computer. If I hear you moving around I'll be out with the whip.'

'The whip?' she asked a little too innocently.

He opened one eye and grinned. 'No,' he teased. 'You wouldn't like it.'

He stretched out in her cosy bed and listened to her rhythmic tapping of the keyboard, feeling his tension rising again already. Crazy. Even by his standards he should be at saturation point, yet here he was randier than ever. Ridiculous.

He gave her just over an hour but then it was time to lay claim to her for a while. He walked up behind her, quietly impressed by the screeds of programming gobbledegook across the big computer screen. She pressed a button and it turned into an incredible graphic interface. Wow.

But she was even more wow.

'I'm going to shower.' He danced his fingertips across her collarbones, bending to kiss the side of her neck.

'Oh.' She sighed deeply.

Seeing her melt was gratifying.

'You want to join me?' He pulled her back towards him so he could kiss lower down her neck.

'Mmm. It'll boost my energy.'

He teased her into the bathroom. It was as amazing as the rest of her flat—antique glass bottles were filled with soaps and lotions and lined up along the shelf, and there were random things in unexpected places. But the shower and basin units were gleaming white, the towels huge and soft and inviting. It was feminine but not fluffy, simple and yet stamped with her quirk. He liked that she'd made a little luxury sanctuary for herself. He also liked it that she ran the water as hot as he did. Watching her enjoy it was almost as sensational as feeling her explode around him. Combining the two was insane.

'Let me.' He rubbed her scalp and twisted her hair into froth covered crazy shapes.

Afterwards she pulled on some clothes and didn't bother doing her hair, just went straight back to park in front of her computer and disappeared off into concentration land. Refusing to feel surplus to requirements, Jack prowled into the kitchen, his stomach telling him sustenance was necessary sooner rather than later. The contents of her cupboards weren't inspiring.

'I'm going to the shop, Kelsi. Anything you want?'

She shook her head and didn't take her eyes from the screen. 'No, I'm fine.'

He walked down to the local supermarket, enjoying the heat of the sun on his back and the prospect of another lazy afternoon in bed. His phone chimed. He checked the screen and grimaced. But this time he had to take the call he'd been avoiding all week.

'Hi, Pete.' His friend and sometimes coach. Calling in coach capacity this time for sure.

'Heard from Tahu.' Pete didn't muck about. 'He said you were cutting some moves on the dance floor the other night.'

'Yeah.' Jack nodded. No denying that.

'The knee's all good now?'

No denying that either. 'A lot better, yeah.'

'So why are you there when the snow's here?'

Good question.

'I thought you said it was going to take a lot more than a couple of weeks?'

That was the 'official' reason he'd given to come back to New Zealand—to take the time to really let his knee heal. But it was all about Kelsi and it always had been. He'd pretended it was the knee for his own sanity—but he knew he was all insane for her. Now, even more.

'Life's gotten a little complicated, Pete,' was all he could say.

'Well, it's your call, but we're here to work if you want to join us.'

'Great. I'll let you know as soon as I do.' He shoved the phone in his pocket and strode out. Frustrated the end loomed so much sooner than he'd wanted to acknowledge.

But it had to end. He had an obligation not just to himself, but to the team sponsors, to the sport itself. He had to get back to work.

This thing between Kelsi and him wasn't anything more than a completion of the fling they'd begun on the beach that day, right? And they'd be friends who'd get on well for the sake of their child.

But he didn't feel 'friendly' towards her. He felt protective and passionate and out of control. He wanted her all the more instead of less. And now his body felt as if it were being torn apart with its conflicting desires.

The only way to deal with it was to put a time limit on it—force it to a close. He'd book his ticket for the end of the week and then maximize these last few days. That would see it out—surely.

He stared sightlessly across the supermarket car park. Decision made. But he didn't want to tell Kelsi. Not just yet. He didn't want to ruin the fragile peace that had built between them. Sleeping together again had been the best thing for them to do, but also the worst—because it had only proven how fantastic they were together. Leaving wasn't going to be that easy at all. Not for him.

But for her? He really wasn't sure. He knew she liked the sex between them, but he didn't know how she really felt about him. Maybe the sex was all it was.

Kelsi was a strong woman—stronger than he'd first thought. And maybe she'd been right that night they'd found out about the baby—she didn't really *need* him.

And she didn't really *want* him.

And he didn't want to ask. For the first time ever in his life, he felt unsure of something. He'd always had such complete confidence—he needed it to do what he did. But understanding Kelsi? He figured he'd find out when he told her he was leaving.

All the more reason to delay doing that a little.

He had to leave believing he was doing the right thing. It was the only way he could. And he was sure he was—he would leave her in the care of the best doctors money could buy, set up in a beautifully restored home...safe.

He didn't bother going into the supermarket after all. His appetite had been crunched.

Kelsi got used to having him in her bed way too easily. The next couple of nights were filled with hedonistic pleasure. Food, fun, frolics. She left work early—hurrying home to see him again. Amazed at the way his hunger inflamed hers.

And he was unbelievably hungry. The stamina of the professional athlete was something to be in awe of. There was no end to it. And it only got hotter.

They lazed across the bed in the evening, surrounded by the initial plans that the architect and Alice the interior decorator had come up with for the redesign of the shell downstairs, laughing about how they'd underestimated her. The design ideas were fantastic.

Finally Kelsi felt excited about the future. With a few twists here and there, the ground floor was going to become a beautiful home. She chose to forget about the flat that would be left upstairs. She chose to ignore all the questions that whispered in the back of her mind. She chose to be swept away by the furious passion he ignited. And he did it so often, with a fierce kind of determination. Keeping them busy—in bed, at play on the skateboard, ever so occasionally letting them sleep.

Jack pulled her close and took her as if he were about to board a ship and face six months' celibacy. Which he was. But it was so much more than this that he was going to miss. He wanted to be with her as the house was put back together, wanted to laugh with her, wanted just to be with her.

Every hour he knew he ought to say something. But every hour he waited made it worse and he couldn't and he was so angry with himself for feeling wrong about something that was right.

That was it—the dream he'd been chasing all his life. He had to go.

And, he figured, how she reacted would be his final answer. Whether she wanted him for something more, or whether this was simply fun sex with a few complications. Complications that for him were becoming increasingly awful.

On Thursday morning Jack was out of bed hours before she was. He'd made her a light breakfast as he had every morning since they'd come together again. But he didn't touch the toast he had on his own plate.

'Kelsi.'

She glanced at him, surprised and silenced by the pale tension in his face.

'I'm flying to Canada on Friday.'

She swallowed back the excess spit that had just surged in her mouth and clamped down on her muscles. Now was not the time for morning sickness. 'Next week?'

'No. I mean tomorrow.'

She reeled in disbelief. Started to giggle—but it died before it bubbled from her lips because he was looking horribly serious. 'When did you book the ticket?'

'Monday.'

So he'd known most of the week? 'Why didn't you tell me?'

He stood up from the table but didn't walk. 'I—'

'Didn't want to.' That was obvious. So only twenty-four hours out from his departure he was landing it on her. She supposed she should be grateful for even that long. It could have been only a couple. She tried not to let panic clutch hold of her. 'How long will you be gone for?'

'Three or four months.'

Wow. She pushed her plate of toast away. Here it was—that future she'd been ignoring. She'd known. His knee was better, he was increasing his exercise.

But she just hadn't believed it. She'd got dazzled by the intensity of their togetherness in the last few days. Had actually started to think his insatiable hunger and need to be near her might mean something more.

But all it had been was him making the most of things before he went away. Having the fun while he could. But he'd have fun over there, too—he was going off with his mates and the snowbunnies and temptation and she was as jealous as hell. And hurt.

He was leaving her. Of course he was leaving her. Had she been so stupid to think that he wouldn't? Yes, she had.

Three or four months meant he'd be away when she had her scan. Her baby's first photo and he wouldn't be there. The first of a million milestones that he'd miss. Just as her father had missed most of hers.

Her baby deserved better.

'Kelsi?'

He was watching her closely. What did he expect—that she'd smile and say OK? It wasn't OK, she wasn't going to make it that easy for him. He wanted everything too easy.

'Um…' Emotion swamped her—pain and anger. Her hands shook and she curled her fingers to stop it. She couldn't get past the shock. And the cold hard truth of his rejection. There wasn't even the tiniest consideration that she might go with him. He was just going to walk out and leave her.

Military wives coped with their men leaving all the time. She knew that. But they had promises and security—and she didn't mean financial.

Emotional. There was no emotional security with Jack.

'Kelsi. You'll be fine. You'll be secure here.'

The air punctured her lungs like shards of glass, deflating the last of her dreams. Did he really think that was all that mattered? What about her heart? Her shaking only worsened and she stood. He'd given her more than that security. He'd given her a child and empty hope. And as payment he'd taken her heart. Only he didn't actually want it.

And that was the horrible reality, wasn't it—he didn't want *her*. Not for anything more than a little fling.

'Our sleeping together again was a really big mistake,' she mumbled.

'It had to happen, Kelsi, you know it did. You can't regret it.'

She didn't look at him. It had to happen? What, they'd had to burn it out? But it wasn't burned out—for her it meant more than ever. Her hands slid to her belly. She regretted everything.

'No,' he said firmly. 'Do *not* regret that.' He walked across the room—halfway to the door already. 'Kelsi, I have to go. This is my life.'

Yeah. His life of travel and adventure and always striving to push his body to the absolute boundaries of ability—all so admirable. Her anger raged—because his 'extreme' life was so safe. And so selfish.

'And this is *mine*. You have to get on with yours, Jack, I

get that. But I have to move on and make a life for myself
and my child.'

He turned back to face her. 'What do you mean?'

'I mean I'm going to get on with it.'

'Without me.'

'You're the one choosing to leave.'

'And there's no coming back? Is that it?'

She nodded fiercely.

'What, this is some kind of ultimatum?' His voice
rose.

Yeah. She wanted to test him—she wanted the truth
in his answer. 'That too big a pill for you, Jack? Someone
asking you for something?'

'You're not asking, you're demanding. And your price
is too high.'

So it was true that words were mightier than the sword—
words could hurt in a way that physical wounds couldn't.
They could poison, and tear apart. She felt as if he'd just
sliced her womb open—exposing her and her baby to extreme vulnerability.

His anger lifted. 'You'd really rather I didn't come back
at all?'

Kelsi clung to the back of the dining chair, gripping it
with both hands. Trying to breathe normally, not take the
great gulps that would give her away—that would acceler-
ate into sobs all too soon. Her brain strained to function,
to protect herself and the tiny life inside her.

'I have to go,' he said too firmly. 'I'm sorry, Kelsi.'

She'd heard those meaningless words before. She'd been
let down so many times before. What was she going to tell
her child? Sorry, honey, but Daddy was too busy getting
his kicks flipping round mountains to call in. 'There's
more to life than tricks and turns and casual sex.'

His muscles bunched. 'This is my job. You have to understand that.'

She could tell this baby that until she was blue in the face but there was always, always that kernel inside that felt the rejection personally. The child would still know that it wasn't a priority. That its father couldn't be bothered—that his work was more important.

Rejection. There was nothing like it.

Kelsi knew the feeling all too well. And even though she had the most wonderful mother who had loved her and supported her—it was still there. There was still that kernel—the one grit of sand that rubbed a tiny spot raw.

Her father hadn't wanted her. And had let her down again and again.

Just as Jack was letting this child down.

He wouldn't change his lifestyle for it. Hotel rooms. A few months here. A few months there. Hell, he wouldn't even be in Christchurch much. When he was in New Zealand he'd be at Karearea Lodge for the season. All this time fixing up the house hadn't been for *him*. His interest in the kitchen design had just been a passing entertainment. The whole thing was simply another project—a job to get done a.s.a.p. so he could get back to the fun bits.

Without her.

And she was such a fool. 'What happened to shared custody?' Her voice rose, wobbling. 'What happened to you taking me to court and fighting me for your right to be a father?'

'You were pushing me out, Kelsi. I had to say something. I had to keep you talking to me. I needed time.'

'For what? To sleep with me some more while you sorted out the house and the money and stuff so then you could go on your merry way feeling like everything was just fabulous? Was this just another little challenge? Was *I* just another challenge?'

'Kelsi, you're not thinking rationally. You're pregnant and you're getting upset.'

'Don't you dare blame my getting upset on pregnancy hormones. You're being a selfish jerk, Jack. Own up to it. And if you want out, then get out for good.'

'No, you're being unreasonable. What do you want from me?' he shouted. 'I'm working as hard as I can to fix this.'

He was throwing some money around and escaping.

'And I'm having a baby,' she shouted back. 'But the timing sucks and you're not the father my child needs. I wanted to give my child what I didn't have. While my mother was fantastic, I know how hard she had to work, the sacrifices she made and what she missed out on because she had me so young and all on her own. I didn't want to let her down by making the same mistake.'

'You were not a mistake,' Jack said quickly. 'Our being together was not a mistake. Our child is not a mistake.'

'No, but our continuing to have any kind of a relationship is.' She slammed the chair into place beneath the table. 'You're walking out, Jack. You can't cope with the idea of settling. Your pattern is fixed and it isn't going to change and that's fine. But I'm not putting my child in a position to have to deal with you popping in and out of its life like a jack-in-the-box.' She looked up at him. 'I know what it's like to be let down time and time again.' She straightened. 'I won't let you do it. I'm going to move out and make my own home for my baby.'

'This is ridiculous Kelsi.' His temper flared and he walked towards her. 'Be honest. This isn't even about the baby. You keep saying it is but it isn't. This is about you. You're mad because I'm leaving you.'

Of all the arrogant, cruel, utterly *correct* things to throw at her. She was furious. Yes, she'd fallen for him. He'd made her fall for him. She wanted him to be with her—to want to be with her. But she'd be damned if she was going to admit that. Not when he so clearly didn't want her the same way.

'Not at all, Jack,' she said, her pride bursting out like New Year's fireworks lighting the sky. 'You can go any time you like. It doesn't bother *me*.'

'Really.' He pulled up taut.

'Of course,' she said, her words brittle and bitchy. 'This is just a fling. It's always been fantasy sex. Physical attraction and all that. You know we're not compatible in any other aspect.'

'Really.' Now he spoke with equally cool precision. 'OK, so if this isn't about you or about us, then it *is* about the baby. But are you sure you're doing such a great job thinking about what will really be of benefit to our child?'

'*I'm* the one putting this child first, Jack.'

'You're putting your own hang-ups first,' he snapped. 'I'm not like your father. I'm not lying—I'm not going to promise something I have no intention of following through on. I'll always step up to my responsibilities but I will do it my way. Yes, a child needs security and consistency but it's also important for him to see his parents happy and fulfilled and achieving their dreams. So the kid learns that it's possible to make dreams come true.'

He walked towards her making his case—articulate, driven, compelling—and slicing the certainty from her.

'So our child won't have a dad in a conventional job or parents in a conventional relationship. So what? Why does that mean I have to be excluded completely from its life?

You don't think the kid might actually be proud of what I do?'

Kelsi folded her arms across her chest and pressed her hands deeper into her sides to stop the hurt escaping.

'I have got a lot I can offer that child—much more than money. I can teach our child passion and in a few years it can travel with me. Imagine the unique experiences I can provide. It'd be a blast.'

She gulped to hold back her gasp—because that really hurt. That hurt more than anything. Because there'd been no mention—no hint even—of her travelling with him. Of her becoming involved in the one true passion of his life.

His mouth compressed at her lack of response. 'I'm the one doing all the running here, Kelsi. I've put my job on hold for the last fortnight so I can sort you out a home and some security—financial and physical. I'm doing all I can to compromise. It's about time you did, too.'

'Two weeks, huh, Jack?' Scorn poured from her. 'How big of you to give it so long. I'm automatically landed with the next nine months. Think on that for a minute, why don't you?'

Jack stalked to the door. 'I won't ever deny that you have the bigger burden, Kelsi. But nor will I let you deny all that I have to contribute as well.'

CHAPTER TWELVE

KELSI operated on sub-normal capacity all day. She'd have to catch up on work in the upcoming weekend again. Theoretically that was no problem, because by then she wouldn't have anyone around to distract her.

But Jack was in her head distracting her now. His words repeated round and round, making her feel really, really bad. She hadn't thought about the full implication of her threat, she'd just hit out because she was hurt.

If she was honest, she'd admit he had a point. He'd been doing everything he could, while she'd stropped around all preoccupied by her insecurities and yearnings for him. She'd protested she was trying to protect her child, but it was all about protecting herself. Her need to carve him from her life was purely for self-preservation. But the baby didn't deserve to miss out on all the good things he had to offer. Lots of people had all kinds of co-parenting arrangements that worked beautifully. She was just going to have to toughen up and get over wanting so much more from him.

But oh, it hurt. How deeply she'd fallen for him. How sky-high her dreams had travelled. They crashed now.

She got home and to her relief he wasn't there. But his presence, his force of will, was evident everywhere—and his incredible productivity. The downstairs flats had

been gutted and the space opened up so the skeleton—
and flaws—could be seen. They just had to fix up all the
failings and finalise the design of the rebuild. He'd been
attentive to her physical security on other levels, too, cooking her dinner night after night, breakfast in the morning.
All this while still driven in his own rehab exercise regime.
There weren't any wild nights on the town or millions
of women. There was only consistent effort—from him.
Getting the job done so he could get back to the good
bits.

And was that so bad of him? Was it wrong to be so
determined to fulfil his dreams and ambitions? People
had to be driven to achieve and the world needed achievers
in all kinds of disciplines. He'd learned the lesson from
his father's choices—that he had to prioritise. And in his
chosen field there was a time limit. Could she really expect
him to give that up?

No. And she didn't want to either.

But maybe it was time for her to think about her own
dreams, too—for her own career, for her own longing to
travel. Couldn't she do that, too?

She walked outside and looked at Jack's makeshift skate
park. The man knew how to make the most out of every
inch of space and of every moment.

She definitely wanted her child to grow up believing
dreams were attainable—its own dreams, not those put
upon it by parents. And maybe Jack was right—maybe
it was work ones that mattered, not relationships. If that
meant her baby saw her set up her own web design company, then great. And if it meant standing on the side of
a mountain and watching Jack hurtle down it faster than
the speed of light, then so be it.

But the streaming ideas didn't fix the glitch in her heart.
Yes, she could start up her own company. Yes, she could

travel. But, fool that she was, she wanted to do all that with him. Yet that wasn't an option that had even crossed his mind.

So while she'd teach her baby about following its dreams, she'd give it a base, too—the home and security she knew were so necessary. They might not be for Jack, but they were for most normal people.

She heard movement outside and glanced out of the window. He was home. She steeled herself. She could suck it up. And she had to start now.

She went down to the yard. He was riding, sending his board sliding across the planks he'd positioned on some make-you-wince angle.

'I was a cow. A complete cow.' She just said it. 'I'm really sorry.'

He jumped off the board and looked at her.

'You're right. You've got to go. It's your job. I'll be fine. This place is going to be fantastic and please understand I do appreciate it. Not having to worry about a home and money is such a big thing, Jack. It really is.'

He ruffled his hair, his hand spread wide as he mussed it up.

'I'll be fine while you're gone and I'll be here when you get back. I was really childish saying I was going to move and shut you out.' She swallowed up all the humble pie. 'You were right, I wasn't thinking about what's best for the baby. I know you won't be like my dad.'

Her heart ached as she said it. He wouldn't be—she knew that in the times that he was around, Jack would be an awesome, involved, super-fun dad. She was just sad he wasn't going to be around all the time. But permanence didn't seem to be in Jack's make-up. He needed to keep on the move, always striving for something just out of reach.

She glanced up to check his reaction. He looked as sombre as she felt.

'We can make it work,' she said, trying to sound sure of it.

'OK,' he said quietly. 'Thank you.'

She blinked.

'What about us?' he asked, moving closer to the jump between them.

Well, he hadn't exactly mentioned 'them' when he'd dropped the 'I'm flying out on Friday' bombshell. But that was the point—there wasn't 'them'. 'You were right about that, too. It isn't about us. It's about the baby.'

He paused. 'I do like you, Kelsi. I like you a lot.'

Yeah, this was where it got messy again. 'I like you, too,' she said quickly. 'And we can be friends, Jack. I know we can be friends.' They could make it all work. But the lovers bit of it wasn't ever meant to last—Jack didn't do relationships like that. Really, his going away was a good thing—it gave her time to try to get over him.

He walked over the raised plank with an easy gait. 'So.' His voice lowered and he looked rueful. 'That's it, then.'

'Yeah,' she said, her voice a mere thread. 'Don't you think?'

For a moment it was there between them—the awareness almost visible. Complicating it again had been the dumbest thing they'd done. But he'd been right about that, too—she couldn't regret it. It had been the experience of a lifetime.

Now she wanted to keep the memories pure. Keep them filled with the sense of fun and freedom—and keep that special boost to her personal confidence. He really had wanted her. And, even though he wanted other things more, it had still been wonderful of him.

But she couldn't do a last kiss or a last lust moment. No

way could she enjoy it if she knew it was the last. No way could her fragile heart handle the finality.

'You're right.' He nodded, moving away to retrieve his skateboard.

'I'm going to get a takeaway for dinner tonight,' she said. 'I really fancy a curry.'

'Sure.' He nodded. 'I've got some people I need to see before I go tomorrow.'

They understood each other, then. No dinner in her flat together. No more time alone. The decisions had been made and agreement reached.

She actually did get a takeaway—for fear he'd notice if she didn't. He was too observant when it came to her eating and sleeping and general welfare. And he actually did go out, too. She lay awake until she heard him get back. She lay awake the rest of the night, too, watching the sky slowly lighten on the day of his departure.

She nibbled on the corner of a plain cracker for breakfast but didn't manage anything more than that. Her nerves were shredded. The sooner she got today over with, the better. So she got ready for work early and then knocked on his door. He opened it immediately—as if he'd been waiting just the other side of it. Fully dressed and clearly ready to go.

'What time is your flight?' She stepped back on the landing, trying to keep it together.

'Mid-morning. Connection to Auckland first.'

She nodded.

'Alice is coming in first thing and I'll get the paperwork done giving you final authority and access to the charge account. Have whatever you want.'

'Thanks,' she muttered. But this house was going to be so empty without him—no matter how beautiful she made

it or how many things she crammed into it, the void would
be huge.

'You take care of yourself.' His blue eyes penetrated—
all concern. 'Make sure you eat well.'

'I promise. I'll take good care of both of us.'

He nodded but didn't relax. In fact his body went rigid.
His hand fisted and he thrust it into his jeans pocket. 'Don't
be mad with me.' His jaw muscles clenched. 'But I made
you an appointment already.'

Jack really didn't want her to be mad or hurt or
unhappy—about any of this mess between them.

Even though he was feeling all three.

But now he knew he couldn't ask her to go with him,
not when she was pregnant and vulnerable—that was a
given. And now he knew she wouldn't accept even if she
wasn't. According to her, they weren't compatible. It really
was just a fling. She didn't want him for anything other
than that and she never had.

That day on the beach when he'd been so careful to tell
her he was going away? She laughed—it hadn't bothered
her in the least.

When he'd turned up on her doorstep? She'd been
cool.

When he'd offered her help? She'd refused.

The only thing they did agree on was the heat between
them. But for the first time in his life he realised he didn't
have any foundation to spring from. Now he knew there
was just this void—so he had to keep moving or he'd come
crashing down.

Now he knew he did want some solid stability. But
it wasn't to be—not with Kelsi. Hell, maybe it was fate
paying him back for all those years 'playing'.

Jack had never known rejection before. It hurt.

But it reinforced the rightness of his decision. He'd go.

He'd work. He'd forget. And when he got back it would all be better—right? He just hoped he could live with it.

He held out the business card as if it were a last challenge.

She took it, quickly skimming the words printed on it.

An obstetric specialist. Kelsi recognised the name—the surgeon was based at the premier private women's health clinic in the city.

'You'll go? It's all paid for in advance.' He actually went paler. 'But I'll be back well before…um…it arrives.'

Kelsi tried not to show her surprise at his steamroller approach to deciding on her care. He was so insistent about this. But she didn't want to fight. Saying goodbye was tough enough.

'I'll go.' She took a step away. 'But I really should get going to work. I don't want to be late.'

'You're walking again.'

'Sure. You were right, it is better. I beat all the banked-up traffic.' Trifling talk was so much easier than dealing with all that was unsaid.

And his answering grin was small, but it was there.

'So, I'll see you in a bit.' Her throat had gone all tight. She turned so she wouldn't have to look at him. So he wouldn't see the waterfalls building in her eyes.

'Right,' he said. 'Soon.'

She walked to the top of the staircase. 'You go get your trick, Jack. Get the gold.' Kelsi really, really wanted that for him. She wanted him to be happy.

He didn't move from his doorway and she was halfway down before he suddenly spoke. 'Kelsi, you can call me if you need me, OK?'

She nodded but didn't turn back. Too busy concentrating on the stairs and on holding back the tears.

She strode fast, out past the over-the-top fencing and along the road that took her to the heart of the city. She ran her thumb across the edge of the obstetric's card. She'd have to diary the appointment in her computer or she'd forget.

A few minutes into the walk—well out of sight of the house—she stopped mid-path to put the card in her purse. She stared at it, her brain ticking. His insistence bothered her. Why was he so concerned for her health? Why had he always made such an effort to cook her all those decent meals. Why did he want her to have a team of specialists for what should be a perfectly normal, healthy pregnancy? What had he seen that made him so nervous? Hadn't his mother ever—?

Her thoughts seized.

His mother.

She sat down at the bus stop a little along from where she'd stopped. She pulled out her iPhone and pulled up the internet for a search. But this time she read the Wikipedia profile instead of being sidetracked by the YouTube clips of all his tricks. This time she hunted through for the bit about his background. Born in China—in a remote mountain village where his father was prepping for an expedition. There it was—just a single line detailing his early arrival, and his mother's death only hours later.

No wonder he was anxious about prenatal care. His mother had died giving birth to him.

Kelsi put her phone in her bag and stood up. Her legs wobbling as she digested that tragedy. Poor Jack. And poor Jack's dad—no wonder he'd put his own adventures on hold. No wonder things were so complicated. And why was it only now that she realised just how much she loved him? She wanted to make it all so much better—to support him however he needed. When she had so much to give, why didn't he want it?

Hardly watching where she was going, she walked, her breathing a little difficult. She definitely should walk more often if she was this unfit. But now the edges of her vision were darkening. Had something gone wrong with her contacts? She shook her head and blinked several times to clear it. Distantly, the thought registered that she wasn't wearing contacts today. But the blackness was all-encroaching now.

And all of a sudden the world went woosh.

'Kelsi? Kelsi?'

Kelsi frowned. Who was calling her?

'Kelsi, are you OK?'

'Alice?' What was the interior decorator doing here? What was Kelsi doing here—flat out on the footpath?

'I think you fainted. Have you hit your head?'

She struggled to sit up. Her stomach rocked as if she was on a catamaran in a storm round Cape Horn. 'Wow,' she said, desperately trying to recover some dignity. 'That was embarrassing.'

'I was driving to the house and saw you keel over. Good thing the traffic was moving so slow or I might have missed you.'

'Yeah.' Kelsi squinted as she tried to force her vision to focus. Her brain felt scrambled.

'You want me to call Jack?' Alice bobbed down, patting Kelsi's shoulder.

'No, don't,' Kelsi said quickly—her mind jerking back to its last-remembered realisation. 'No. Please don't bother him. This is just nothing.'

If he heard about this, he might freak out. He might postpone going. And as much as she really wanted that, she knew it wasn't right. She didn't want him to stay here because of fears—she didn't want him to be trapped. That would be worse than anything.

Alice frowned. 'You really don't look so good, Kelsi. You're very pale.'

'I'm always pale.' Kelsi stretched her lips into something like a smile. 'Look, I'll go into that café just there. I forgot to have breakfast, that's all. I'm fine. Really, I am.'

'Are you sure?'

'Oh, yes.' Forcing animation into her answer, she then went for distraction. 'I had such a great time looking over your ideas folder for the house. You've got some great things in there. I was so pleased you picked up on some of the old features.'

Alice's expression lightened. Kelsi smiled harder and talked for another few minutes about the project, carefully getting to her feet and trying to hide how huge the effort was.

Alice walked with her to the door of the café but then glanced at her watch. 'I'd better get going. Are you sure you're all right now?'

'Absolutely.' She couldn't let her go without a final plea. 'Don't mention it to him, will you? It's so embarrassing and he'll worry unnecessarily. You know how men sometimes do...' Kelsi trailed off and smiled in the hope Alice would enter into the sisterhood-sticks-together spirit.

'Sure.' Alice finally smiled back. 'I'll be in touch with you next week and we can arrange a trip to look at some fabric swatches, OK?'

'That'd be great.'

Kelsi went to the counter and ordered hot chocolate and hot toast. As she made herself eat, she hoped that Alice would keep her word. Jack had to get on that plane. Nothing could stand in his way.

* * *

Jack aimlessly wandered about the big bare space downstairs. He'd ordered a taxi to get him to the airport but as it was a domestic flight first he didn't have to be there hours in advance. And he didn't have much baggage to check through because his snowboard gear was in Canada already.

He ran his hand along the pared-back walls. When he got back, most of the work would be done and the house would look completely different. Whole again, not broken up into pieces that were too small. He couldn't wait to see what Kelsi did with it—to lie on a sofa and stare at whatever collection of disparate objects she'd put together. She'd make it a really nice home.

Her home, he reminded himself. Not his.

He turned his back on the room, jogging upstairs to grab his bag—suddenly needing to grip on to his future. He buzzed the taxi company and got them to pick him up immediately—leaving the signed forms for Alice to collect when she got in. He didn't really need to see her, Kelsi would give her all the instructions.

At the airport he picked up a coffee and a paper and paced around the boarding lounge, telling himself everything had worked out for the best. It was good they'd scaled back to a manageable level of friendship. All very sensible.

At last his flight was called. And all of a sudden he felt more physically incapacitated than when his knee had crunched out the wrong way.

He couldn't move. Didn't want to. His whole body ached as if he had some virulent flu. And then it went hard because all he could think of was Kelsi, Kelsi, Kelsi.

Mortified at his sudden regression into out of control teen boy, he forced his feet to get him onto the plane. She didn't want him. It was just sex. That was all he was walking away from and he'd get back in the game with someone else sometime.

Now his stomach felt sick.

Cold sweat slithered over his body. He was being so stupid. They'd sorted an arrangement that would work for the baby. Kelsi had a home that would soon be wonderful, she was as safe and secure as he could make her. Everything was as good as it could possibly be. He was free to go back to the snow and not have to worry. So why did he feel so rotten?

He squashed himself into his seat. He'd feel better once he got there. He closed his eyes and visualised the mountain. Imagined a helicopter ride up to the top and looking down on the perfect virgin powder ready for him to shred.

He opened his eyes again and sighed. The thrill would come back. He just had to get where the challenge was.

His gut twinged painfully. There was a challenge here, too. A challenge he was walking away from. Not that little baby. But the beautiful mother—the beyond-all-boundaries trick who put pepper in his pulse.

His ride with Kelsi most definitely had not been easy— but wicked for sure. And when had he ever walked away from a challenge that posed such risk?

Since when was he such a chicken?

He closed his eyes again to picture a slope. But instead, Kelsi's teasing smile danced in front of him. Excitement surged. He gripped the armrests as he realised the thrill wasn't just physical—it was total, mind and soul.

The elderly woman seated beside him gave him a cold look.

He couldn't bring himself to care because his heart had suddenly grown too big for his chest and it was pounding too hard.

He *was* walking away from the biggest challenge of his life. He, who thought nothing of putting himself in physical danger, had been too scared to put his heart on the line. To tell her the *truth*. He needed to tell her about his mother, and about how he felt and what he wanted from her—as in everything. He couldn't hide it any more, not from himself or from her. He had to be honest. That was all that mattered now.

His body ached all the more as he thought about baring himself so brutally. Would she respond in kind? Did she ever?

No. He almost laughed—but it hurt too much.

Kelsi covered up all the time—literally and emotionally. It was her specialty. He bent his head, inwardly groaning at his blindness. He already knew she'd lied—like when she'd said she hadn't had morning sickness but he'd heard her. She'd been all defensive pride. She was terrified of getting too close, because she was even more terrified of rejection.

He tensed up as he thought of that. So had those devastating words been lies, too? When she'd said his leaving didn't bother her? Had she been rejecting him before he could reject her? Like some warped method of self-defence?

He winced—both hopeful and devastated. She'd been hurt and he'd been hurt and they'd both been blind to each other.

Yet so much of what she'd said had been true—maybe he was selfish, and, yes, until now he'd never wanted to settle. The thought of being stuck in one place still made his blood bubble. But the security he sought now wasn't of place, but of heart.

She was his home. *She* was the foundation that had been missing for ever.

He'd meant it when he'd said he had a lot to offer their child. And he had so much to offer her, too: his loyalty, his life, his love—and that was just for starters. And he wanted them both to be proud of him. The satisfaction would last for ever if he brought it home to share with the ones he loved. It would make everything worthwhile. And he wanted to support them in the same way—as they realised hopes and dreams and dealt with disappointments.

Way too late he realised he wanted it all with them. With her.

The bad feeling was worsening now. Had he suddenly got claustrophobic? Because he was finding it hard to breathe in this too-tiny cabin. His heart rate skipped faster. He straightened out his aching knee—having to twist on an angle to do it. The action earned him another frown from the woman seated next to him. He hated the fact the airline had cut first class from the domestic routes. He needed the space to stretch out today. Or to fidget.

Actually maybe it would be better if he just got off the plane. He really wasn't feeling so good. But the light went on above his head and the little bell chimed. He obeyed the instruction and fastened his seat belt. It was too late now. It was time for take-off.

CHAPTER THIRTEEN

KELSI sat at work 'til late because she wanted to delay going back to the big, empty house. But eventually she had to move—she didn't want it to get dark before she walked home. The late summer sun still warmed the path but she felt cold and alone. She put her hand in her pocket and toyed with her phone. She had to talk to someone. And there really was only the one person who could come close to understanding.

She was silly for being so afraid to tell her. Now she realised there was nothing to be ashamed of—she loved the father of her baby, she wanted her baby and loved it already, too. Their situation might not ever be perfect, but nothing ever was, right? It could all be OK. She was proud of Jack, would welcome him into her child's life whenever he was back. But she had to let him go—that was what loving him meant. And he was worthy of her love.

And her baby deserved all her pride.

So she finally phoned her mother.

A few tears, some laughter. A lot of understanding—and excitement, too. They talked almost her entire walk home. Relieved and emotional and alternately happy and despairing, Kelsi agreed to go and visit her mum soon.

As she turned down her street she put her phone away. Her pace slowed as she saw movement behind the fencing—up by the house. Had one of the builders stayed later to clean up something? The padlock on the chain was open, the gate ajar—waiting for her return.

He was sweeping dust from the deck. Tall and fit and undeniably Jack.

Her heart squeezed with joy. And then disappointment smashed it.

'Alice told you.' She was so happy to see him again but he wasn't here for any of the right reasons. It hurt even more. 'Jack, you need to go.'

She needed him to go *now*. Before she threw herself at him. His leaving was the worst thing that could happen to her but she had to let him go. He wasn't capable of living the kind of life she needed. He didn't want the same things from her as she wanted from him. She'd been right, they weren't compatible in any of the things that mattered. But she loved him and he needed to be free.

He carefully leaned the broom against the wall. 'I'm not going.'

She carefully climbed the steps, forcing herself to keep her emotions in check. 'But you love shredding the mountains. It's your life.'

'Life changes.' He shrugged. 'So do priorities.'

Damn it, she didn't want fear to stop him from achieving. 'But—'

'I can't win with you, can I?' He suddenly blew up. 'God, I actually thought you might be pleased to see me. But no matter what I do—the compromises I try to make— it's never right for you. I'm not right.' He took a step towards her, tension rolling off him. 'What do I have to do for you? What do I have to do for you to want me?'

Desperately she held back her heart. 'I don't want you to be someone you're not.'

'But you can't be with the person I am. I have no choice

but to change, Kelsi. I'll do whatever I have to do, to be with you.'

'Look, I'm fine, Jack,' Kelsi said, knowing she couldn't believe what he was saying, knowing this was simply concern. 'The baby is fine. I don't know what Alice told you but—'

'I haven't talked to Alice,' he interrupted roughly. 'Whatever she wants can wait.'

Kelsi frowned. 'But this is about the baby—'

'You still don't trust me, do you?' he roared. 'How the hell do I get you to trust me?' Furious, he stalked over to her, yelling in her face. 'This isn't about the baby. This is about *you*. And *me*. And my inability to leave you.'

'What?'

'I don't want to go without you, OK? I don't want to leave *you*.'

'But—'

'Kelsi, I want to be with you more than I want anything in my life. More than anything. So I'm staying.' He grabbed her shoulders with hard fingers. 'I can't have you come with me because I cannot cope with the idea of you being on the road while pregnant. That's just not something I can handle. My mum died having me, Kelsi. They were halfway up a mountain and I came early and she haemorrhaged and there wasn't the care she needed. So I need to know you're in a city and near a hospital and safe. And, as irrational as that may be, you're just going to have to let me away with it because that's one thing I just can't get past, so don't expect me to. I can't take you any place remote and vulnerable. It's just not going to happen, OK?'

'OK.' She nodded, her limbs trembling. 'I get that one.'

'Well, can you get the rest a little quicker, please? Because I'm going insane here.'

'What's the rest?'

'I love you. I love you. I love you.'

His arms were tight around her and his words ran over each other, all over her, and she couldn't see through the sheen of tears, couldn't breathe because her face was pressed hard into his shoulder.

'Jack?' she gasped, her fingers clutching at his shirt as she tried and failed to comprehend this magic.

Eventually he took her hands in his, not quite calmly saying it again. And more. 'We'll stay here until the baby arrives. Then I can prep for the season in Karearea. You and the baby can stay in the lodge with me. Is that OK? Do you think you could want that?'

'Oh—'

His mouth moved over hers—not giving her the chance to answer. The kiss was wet and didn't work well because she was sobbing and shaking but it didn't matter. He was here and he was real and not only was he not leaving, he wasn't letting her go.

Finally he lifted his head and looked her directly in the eyes. 'You're so precious to me,' he said. 'You're everything to me. And it scares me so much. So much more than any sheer slope.'

Kelsi still couldn't move, still couldn't believe. 'Is it me or is it the baby?'

'Kelsi, I came back for you. It's always been you. Before we even knew about the baby, it was you.'

Her stunned-mullet reaction made him haul her closer and speak even faster. 'From the moment I saw you, you got into my heart and I need you there. I should have known at the time. You're the whole reason I came back from Canada—it wasn't my stupid knee. It was you. And now, yes, the baby, too. I've got you both and I never knew how much I needed you.'

'But I don't want you to ruin your life.' Her tears streamed. 'I don't want you giving up something you love so much because you want to do the right thing.'

'This isn't the right thing. This is the *only* thing. I can't go. My happiness depends on staying. I'm still the same selfish jerk. Holding on to you is the most selfish thing I've ever done.' He bent his head, speaking in even more of a rush than before. 'You're so strong, Kelsi. And courageous—far more courageous than me. And you're hard-working and talented and funny and I love everything about you.' He pulled her closer and she could feel how he was shaking, too.

'You won't get bored?' she asked, painfully aware of how pitiful the question was, but she couldn't stop herself from asking it. 'You're a man who loves a challenge, Jack.'

'You know what?' he said softly. 'I finally get what Dad meant when he said he had challenges bigger and more rewarding than Everest. *I* was his challenge, Kelsi. As you're mine. And our baby will be our challenge to deal with together. It's so exciting, don't you think? No bigger challenge than that. And we'll face it together.'

'But I don't want you giving up everything. That's not fair.'

'It's just this season—and it's half over already. I can train in the gym and then pick up again come the New Zealand winter. I'll still have to travel. And I'm still going for the Olympics and my gold medal. But maybe by then you and the baby could come with me?'

She crumpled and hid her face in his chest again. 'I want to. I want to cheer you on and be there for you—oh, everywhere. I want your kind of excitement. I want the adventure. I wanted to change my life for you, too, Jack.' Her voice broke. 'I just didn't think you wanted me to.'

'Kelsi…' he groaned. 'You can trust me, darling. I'm never going to leave you, I'm never going to let you down. So don't ever hold back from me—don't hide. You don't have to protect yourself any more, because it's my job to protect you.'

Fighting back the sobs, she mumbled the plan she'd so secretly dreamed of. 'I can work anywhere,' she said quickly. 'Wireless internet, you know? I can freelance. It'll be fun.'

'*After* the baby's born. You're staying within five miles of a hospital until then.'

'OK.' And she finally felt the warmth as it sank in. He was here. He really was here for her. He wanted her and together they could have it all.

'And you know we have a lot to do in the next few months. We have to get this place fixed up.'

She nodded, her smile unstoppable.

'And maybe…' His voice trailed off and he cleared his throat. 'Neither of us are particularly mainstream, Kelsi. But do you think you could cope with something as conventional as marriage?'

She looked, saw the flicker of uncertainty, and her confidence soared. 'I'm more of a traditionalist than you think, Jack Greene. Because I don't class that as a proposal.'

He laughed and pressed a quick kiss to her mouth, then dropped to his knees before her. 'You like me like this, don't you?' he teased.

'You know I do.' She cupped her hands on his jaw—feeling the stubble, the strength, seeing the sudden flash of tenderness, passion, truth in his eyes.

'Please marry me, Kelsi.' He wasn't joking now.

'Are you sure?'

His groan was pure desperation. 'Kelsi—'

'Yes,' she whispered. 'Yes, please.'

He scooped her up swiftly, easily, shouldering the door open and taking the stairs two at a time.

'Watch your knee,' she said breathlessly, clinging to him.

He laughed and barged into her bedroom. But when he laid her on the bed his expression went serious again—and sorry.

'I got on the plane and pretty much freaked out. I'm so sorry I thought I could walk out on you. On this.'

This time the kiss was sublime. This time the kiss was endless and infinitely tender. This time he was the one who trembled—as if the reality of what had almost happened hit him. That he'd almost lost her.

He pulled her close and she sensed his urgency—the conflicting needs tearing him apart as he tried to stay gentle while desperate to be with her as deeply and as quickly as possible.

'Relax,' she soothed as she kissed him back with as much love as she had in her.

'I'm sorry,' he choked. 'I'm so sorry.'

'Shh.' She kissed him again and kept kissing him so he could no longer agonise.

His face flushed, his fingers trembling as he reached out to her. And so she welcomed him—opening herself up so he could access every last inch of her heart and soul. She smiled as he claimed his spot in the very centre of her. He muttered her name over and over, the words of love over and over. He couldn't hold them back and she couldn't hide how they affected her.

In his arms she was bared completely, at her most vulnerable.

And never so safe.

* * *

They lay quietly for a few moments, recovering from the overload of sensation and emotion. And then he stretched out with a sigh and a smile of absolute satisfaction. 'We really need to think about designing the master bedroom.'

'Where's that going to be?' Kelsi frowned as she tried to concentrate. Now she thought about it, she hadn't seen it on the plans.

'Right about here,' he said, watching her closely. 'I'm going to take out your flat. You don't mind?'

'No.' Happiness ran through her veins faster than the blood he'd already heated. The house would be whole, just as they'd be whole—together. 'It'll be fun creating something new.'

His expression lit up as he gave her a huge smile. 'Maybe we should build our own place on Karearea, too, rather than staying at the lodge.'

'You're going to build homes everywhere now?'

'Sure. Now I have the family to keep in them.'

And that sweet statement so totally deserved a reward.

'Have you told your mother about the baby yet?' he asked when he could speak again—quite some time later.

'Yes,' Kelsi said softly.

He tilted her face so he could see it clearly. 'We'll go and see her in person soon, OK? I can't wait to meet her.'

Her eyes were watering ridiculously now. Because he would—she knew with absolute certainty that she could count on him.

'Kelsi?' He chuckled but wiped the tears away with gentle thumbs. A pointless exercise because it only made more tears flood her eyes and tumble down her cheeks.

'Hormones, right?' he asked.

'Totally.' She sniffed. 'Not.' She threw her arms around him. 'I love you, Jack Greene.'

He rolled so he could be the cushion for her head—and her heart. His sigh long and relieved. 'Thank goodness.'

He brushed her hair and tears back and held her until the last of her doubts drained away. And at last she believed in him and in herself.

In each other's arms, they'd finally found home.

Coming Next Month

from **Harlequin Presents®**. Available April 26, 2011.

Coming Next Month

from **Harlequin Presents® EXTRA.** Available May 10, 2011.

Visit www.HarlequinInsideRomance.com
for more information on upcoming titles!

REQUEST YOUR FREE BOOKS!

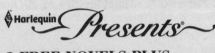 

2 FREE NOVELS PLUS
2 FREE GIFTS!

YES! Please send me 2 FREE Harlequin Presents® novels and my 2 FREE gifts (gifts are worth about $10). After receiving them, if I don't wish to receive any more books, I can return the shipping statement marked "cancel." If I don't cancel, I will receive 6 brand-new novels every month and be billed just $4.05 per book in the U.S. or $4.74 per book in Canada. That's a saving of at least 15% off the cover price! It's quite a bargain! Shipping and handling is just 50¢ per book in the U.S. and 75¢ per book in Canada.* I understand that accepting the 2 free books and gifts places me under no obligation to buy anything. I can always return a shipment and cancel at any time. Even if I never buy another book, the two free books and gifts are mine to keep forever.   106/306 HDN FC55

Name   (PLEASE PRINT)

Address   Apt. #

City   State/Prov.   Zip/Postal Code

Signature (if under 18, a parent or guardian must sign)

Mail to the **Reader Service:**
IN U.S.A.: P.O. Box 1867, Buffalo, NY 14240-1867
IN CANADA: P.O. Box 609, Fort Erie, Ontario L2A 5X3

Not valid for current subscribers to Harlequin Presents books.

**Are you a current subscriber to Harlequin Presents books
and want to receive the larger-print edition?
Call 1-800-873-8635 or visit www.ReaderService.com.**

* Terms and prices subject to change without notice. Prices do not include applicable taxes. Sales tax applicable in N.Y. Canadian residents will be charged applicable taxes. Offer not valid in Quebec. This offer is limited to one order per household. All orders subject to credit approval. Credit or debit balances in a customer's account(s) may be offset by any other outstanding balance owed by or to the customer. Please allow 4 to 6 weeks for delivery. Offer available while quantities last.

Your Privacy—The Reader Service is committed to protecting your privacy. Our Privacy Policy is available online at www.ReaderService.com or upon request from the Reader Service.

We make a portion of our mailing list available to reputable third parties that offer products we believe may interest you. If you prefer that we not exchange your name with third parties, or if you wish to clarify or modify your communication preferences, please visit us at www.ReaderService.com/consumerchoice or write to us at Reader Service Preference Service, P.O. Box 9062, Buffalo, NY 14269. Include your complete name and address.

*With an evil force hell-bent on destruction,
two enemies must unite to find a truth that turns
all-too-personal when passions collide.*

*Enjoy a sneak peek in Jenna Kernan's next installment
in her original* TRACKER *series, GHOST STALKER,
available in May, only from Harlequin Nocturne.*

"Who are you?" he snarled.

Jessie lifted her chin. "Your better."

His smile was cold. "Such arrogance could only come from a Niyanoka."

She nodded. "Why are you here?"

"I don't know." He glanced about her room. "I asked the birds to take me to a healer."

"And they have done so. Is that *all* you asked?"

"No. To lead them away from my friends." His eyes fluttered and she saw them roll over white.

Jessie straightened, preparing to flee, but he roused himself and mastered the momentary weakness. His eyes snapped open, locking on her.

Her heart hammered as she inched back.

"Lead who away?" she whispered, suddenly afraid of the answer.

"The ghosts. Nagi sent them to attack me so I would bring them to her."

The wolf must be deranged because Nagi did not send ghosts to attack living creatures. He captured the evil ones after their death if they refused to walk the Way of Souls, forcing them to face judgment.

"Her? The healer you seek is also female?"

"Michaela. She's Niyanoka, like you. The last Seer of Souls and Nagi wants her dead."

Jessie fell back to her seat on the carpet as the possibility of this ricocheted in her brain. Could it be true?

"Why should I believe you?" But she knew why. His black aura, the part that said he had been touched by death. Only a ghost could do that. But it made no sense.

Why would Nagi hunt one of her people and why would a Skinwalker want to protect her? She had been trained from birth to hate the Skinwalkers, to consider them a threat.

His intent blue eyes pinned her. Jessie felt her mouth go dry as she considered the impossible. Could the trickster be speaking the truth? Great Mystery, what evil was this?

She stared in astonishment. There was only one way to find her answers. But she had never even met a Skinwalker before and so did not even know if they dreamed.

But if he dreamed, she would have her chance to learn the truth.

Look for GHOST STALKER by Jenna Kernan,
available May only from Harlequin Nocturne,
wherever books and ebooks are sold.

Harlequin® Romance

*Don't miss an irresistible new trilogy
from acclaimed author*

SUSAN MEIER

IN THE BOARDROOM

Greek Tycoons become devoted dads!

Coming in April 2011
The Baby Project

Whitney Ross is terrified when she becomes guardian
to a tiny baby boy, but everything changes when
she meets dashing Darius Andreas, Greek tycoon
and now a brand-new daddy!

Second Chance Baby (May 2011)
Baby on the Ranch (June 2011)

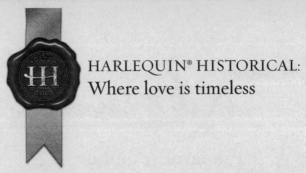

HARLEQUIN® HISTORICAL:
Where love is timeless

Claimed by the Highlander

FROM FAN-FAVOURITE AUTHOR
MICHELLE WILLINGHAM

SCOTLAND, 1305

Warrior Bram MacKinloch returns to the Scottish Highlands to retrieve his bride—and the dowry that will pay for his brother's freedom.

His wayward wife, Nairna MacPherson, hopes for an annulment from her estranged husband who has spent most of their marriage in prison.

But the boy she married years ago has been irrevocably changed by his captivity. His body is scarred, nightmares disturb his sleep, but most alarming of all is *her* overwhelming desire to kiss every inch of his battle-honed body....

**Available from Harlequin® Historical
May 2011**

Look out for more from the MacKinloch clan coming soon!

Harlequin®

A *Romance* FOR EVERY MOOD™

www.eHarlequin.com

Fan favorite author
TINA LEONARD
is back with
an exciting new miniseries.

Six bachelor brothers are given a challenge—
get married, start a big family and whoever does
so first will inherit the famed Rancho Diablo.
Too bad none of these cowboys is marriage material!

Callahan Cowboys:
Catch one if you can!

The Cowboy's Triplets (May 2011)
The Cowboy's Bonus Baby (July 2011)
The Bull Rider's Twins (Sept 2011)
Bonus Callahan Christmas Novella! (Nov 2011)
His Valentine Triplets (Jan 2012)
Cowboy Sam's Quadruplets (March 2012)
A Callahan Wedding (May 2012)